RASPBERRY RIVER

Raspberry River

Howard D. Paap

NORTH STAR PRESS OF ST. CLOUD, INC.
St. Cloud, Minnesota

Illustrations: Corinne A. Dwyer

ISBN: 0-87839-263-7
ISBN-13: 978-0-87839-263-6

First Edition: September 2007

Printed in the United States of America

Published by
North Star Press of St. Cloud, Inc.
P.O. Box 451
St. Cloud, Minnesota 56302

northstarpress.com

1 2 3 4 5 6 7 8 9 10

For
Max, Beth, and Keller

Acknowledgements

Thanks to friend Art Ode for reading this manuscript in its entirety and offering many thoughtful comments. Thanks to Corinne Dwyer of North Star Press for adding the excellent drawings. To Bud, Chuck, Sid, Joe, and the rest in that circle of others on that campus so long ago, thanks for being there. To Ray and Anne Smith goes gratitude for the years of suburban neighborliness. A son's gratitude goes to Mother, who knew intimately what work is and whose chickens those really were. To Pa Trost, who did the lion's share of the work on those farms season after season and never once uttering a word of complaint—Thank you!. *Milgwech* to all those good folks who call the Red Cliff Ojibwe Reservation home, and thanks to Herb Frank for his sincere friendship and genuine *joie de vivre*. His wonderful, infectious approach to life is something to behold! But finally to Marlene goes the biggest thank you of all.

ഇ • ൠ

Previously Published

"Red Bird's Lament" (from "Three Suburban Pieces") was published in
    Storystone, Volume 4, Number 1, Winter, 1985.

"Enlightenment" was published as "Enlightenment" ("The Buddha and
    the Mums") in *Communitas: Journal of Ideas and Letters*, Volume II,
    Number 2, Spring 1989.

"Butternuts" was published in *Inner Mission*, Summer 1984.

ℬ • ℭ

Prologue

These short fiction pieces attempt to say something about the America I have experienced over most of my lifetime. They suggest three different foci: rural, urban, and that of the Indian reservation. I have experienced all three, and here I raise questions about assumptions and realities found in each. Were the eighteenth- and nineteenth-century European social thinkers correct when they posited the notion of a natural human movement from wilderness to farm, and then on to the city? If so, what changes are made inside us when we make this move? Furthermore, if, as the theorists felt, after many thousands of years, we have finally achieved the city, what comes now? Surely the urban life cannot be the end of the line. Where do we go from here? And, importantly, where does the world of the Indian reservation belong in this schematic? Do Indian reservations call this model for on-going human life into question? Could it be that the fabled gleaming city on the hill was not the completion of the human trek all along?

These are stories that try to show that beneath all our apparent differences, we are still struggling with the same needs that confronted our ancestors. Deep inside our personal lives the same symbols and metaphors they dealt with are at play, twisting and turning throughout our days and nights as we attempt to love, and live with, each other, and, just as clearly, as we attempt to love and live with ourselves.

Finally, and most importantly, the natural world that the ancients experienced still surrounds us each day, and like a good friend, silently watches and waits for us to do the right thing.

Howard D. Paap

Bayfield, Wisconsin
September 2007

৵ • ৶

Table of Contents

TOWN

COUNTRY

RESERVATION

❧ Town ❧

❧ 1 ❧

The Good Life

*If we're lucky we may discover a story
that teaches us to abhor our old romance
with conquest and possession.*

—William Kittredge, 1987

IT WAS A BRIGHT, WINDY, luscious, not-many-more-like-this-before-winter day. Yes, it's great, he thought, as he looked down at his Nike-clad feet moving almost effortlessly on the path beside the lake. They were, he fantasized, connected to two steel rods on the well-greased wheels of a locomotive, coming forward, now one, now its partner, again and again. These things come in sets, he mused, two at a time. Then his feet were like the pairs of mallards lazily feeding in the shallows near shore; like daylight and darkness, like male and female. Hegel was right: the dialectic was everywhere. Even life itself cannot be understood without its constant, dark companion running at its side.

Petrie Wilson was out on his morning run, this time along the north shore of the lake. His thin figure, his medium stature, his brown, short-cropped hair, and his light complexion all served to make him

1

common in appearance, just one of many runners who used the path most mornings.

But today it was different. For some reason, life filled him this day. It was fall, and maybe he was preoccupied with the darkness of the coming winter, but today he deeply felt *life*. The lake often did this to him. Was it the water? Was it the lush foliage near the shoreline that, even in the hottest and driest times of summer retained its freshness as its many hidden roots reached to the lake? These trees and bushes were a deep green that rivaled the even deeper verdure of the manicured and enriched lawns that led up to the posh lakeside homes. All this luxuriance was matched by the extravagance of the houses themselves, standing back from the water on higher ground, sheltered by towering hardwoods and thick green conifers. Showpieces to be sure, the size and opulence of these pricey houses matched Petrie's gusto this morning. Things were going well in the world.

It was a scheduled eight-mile day and the miles sped by. However, he began to feel heavier at the sixth mile. Countering the signs of fatigue, he pushed a bit harder to overcome the heaviness, to run through it. When, during the seventh mile, he heard the car's horn, he was glad to see his friend and neighbor, Arnie Sackforth, who obviously wanted to stop and talk. The runner was inwardly grateful for the excuse to slow his stride.

"What're you doing later today?" Arnie shouted through the rolled down window.

Petrie knew Arnie had something planned that involved both of them. He responded, still striding, although with less speed, beside the slowly moving, rusting Ford Taurus, by shouting "Why? What's up?"

"Well, I'd sure like to test that motor."

"Sounds good. Let me run home and shower. I'll be at the dock in a little while."

Within an hour they were at Arnie's dilapidated dock in the weedy little channel that ran beside his lot, about a block from the lake.

"Give me a hand here. Let's tip this over and slide it into the water," Arnie said, motioning to an up-turned, faded, light-colored wooden boat lying amongst the weeds at the side of the channel.

"Look at this," Petrie said, surprised. "Jenny Wren must have raised a family under here."

"I'll be darned. How do you know it's a wren's nest?" Arnie asked.

"I don't, but some bird hatched a brood under this thing."

"Well, at least somebody used the boat this summer. That's funny a bird would build on the ground like that, what with the mink and all around here."

"Mink?" Petrie responded. "What mink? Didn't they leave back in the 1860s with the Dakota? About the only animals prowling these shores are *Homo sapiens* suburbanensis and spindly-legged, bug-eyed French poodles that leave little chocolate mountains for me to step on with my new Nikes."

They slid the boat into the water, mounted the small outboard and were soon out of the channel, onto the lake. A strong, gusty but warm wind came right toward them out of the southwest.

"D'you think the old tub can take these waves?" Petrie asked, sitting amidships on the splintery wooden bench seat as he slipped his arm into a faded orange life jacket. Arnie, steering the little seven-horse Montgomery Ward outboard, sat in the stern, wearing an old preserver that once had been yellow but had sun-baked to a dirty white.

"Hey, Pete," he smiled, "don't call it that. This is a genuine Amundson boat, handmade from the finest selected cedar. Look at that Scandinavian craftsmanship," he went on, pointing to the hull with his mouth and chin.

"What craftsmanship?" Petrie chided. "I can't see it under these five layers of paint—no, wait," he continued, leaning forward and chipping a dried bubble away, "there are seven layers here."

The boat was a fourteen-foot rowboat that really had been made at the old Amundson Boat Works that used to stand at the edge of the little cove on the west end of the lake. All that was left of the factory was a cement slab, now used as a parking spot for nightly trysts, usually littered with plastic, paper, and aluminum cans. Water-worshippers came some evenings just at dusk to sit in their vehicles and commune, their stereo systems sometimes booming deep, resonating bass notes audible blocks away.

The boat was expertly made, but it had been neglected for years. Its hull was covered outside with fiberglass, inside with the several coats of paint, each showing here and there as it peeked out from the overlaying chipped layers. The last coat was a light green, but four other shades of that color were visible, along with sporadic pink spots, and at the bow a loud, bright splash of yellow leaped at the onlooker.

The craft settled into the lake and moved slowly out, straight into the waves as if it were truly glad to be on the water after a long, dry summer. Petrie had to admit it was a well-made boat. It felt at home in the water.

"This motor sounds good," Arnie commented, turning his head to glance back at it. "Those monkeys at the marina wanted $85.00 to fix it. They said it needed clutch work, a new gear, and Lord knows what. I told them to forget it and took it to the vocational school, but they were backlogged for months. They said I should have brought it in January or February. So, I finally took it to old Joe Swenson at the gas station. He brought it back a week later and charged me ten bucks. He said it just needed a good cleaning."

"Rip-off city," Petrie muttered, looking across the lake at the marina, shaking his head. "Joe is one of the few real people left in this town. You know, for years and years I've never seen him get upset, or say anything negative about anyone, except once. That was last week when I stopped for gas. He'd been working on a big Lexus and came to the till, wiping his hands on a rag. I remarked about the big car and its owner, and he looked up the way he does—you know the way he looks at you, how he tilts his head down and peers over his glasses—well, he gave me that look and said, 'Ya, it's an expensive one all right, but maybe if they had less money they'd be a little more friendly.'"

Arnie listened as he often did when his friend seemed to forget that he was not in the lecture hall, telling students about life.

"But I worry about Joe Swenson," Petrie went on. "When Millie died last year—they were married for a helluva long time—he was in the station the next morning, quiet but just as nice as could be. Since she's gone he's all alone, and an old guy like that who's lived in this town all his life has to have misgivings about how things have changed. His hometown's become a haven for the wealthy, and all the time he still works for a low wage. Sometimes I wonder what he really thinks, what he really feels." Arnie kept on listening, looking out over the water as the cleaned motor, almost as old as the boat, hummed quietly and steadily behind him.

It was a Monday morning, the last day of August. The public schools had opened, and the lake with its shoreline, was deserted. Arnie and Petrie were on the faculty at the local community college and still had one more day of freedom before they, too, returned to the all-staff meetings that started each fall term. Without putting their feelings to voice, it was clear that they hoped to savor the day, to ring it dry.

"We've got the whole lake to ourselves," Petrie said. "The eight-to-fivers are at their drill presses. Hey," he continued, looking around, "this is going to be a nice cruise. Good thing this motor needed testing." They both chuckled, knowing that Joe Swenson had checked it out on the lake last week. Joe never let motors go back without a test run. The whole town knew the story, knew how Joe looked for excuses to get out on the water.

"The Dakota used to come up here for ricing back in the thirties," Petrie went on. "Ruth Landes wrote about it in her book on Dakota culture, but I don't think there's any wild rice left on the lake today." Then after a quiet pensive pause he said, "I wonder if the white bears are still here. They're supposed to be around, ya know, down there somewhere. Last spring an Ojibwe medicine man told me they were still here. Do you know these things?" he asked, glancing back to his partner.

5

"Never heard these stories," Arnie responded, not taking his eyes off the lake as he steered the boat. His answer told of his lack of interest. Then turning his gaze to starboard he said, "Look out there—that thing's adrift."

"Let's bring it in," Petrie said, studying the dark image of a sailboat in the middle of the lake at its deepest part, lazily bouncing on the waves. The sails had not been raised, and a small outboard motor was evident at its stern but not running.

"Isn't there anyone on it?" Arnie asked as he pointed the old boat to it.

"I don't think so, but it's hard to tell the way it's bobbing. I don't see an anchor line."

They were soon upon the boat and discovered a sleek, new, small sailboat, unoccupied, showing no signs of recent use. Arnie tied a yellow nylon line to its bow, the other end to his boat's stern.

"We'll take it to the public dock in the park. I'll call the DNR when we get back."

"Rescue at sea—make way for the Coast Guard," Petrie kidded, as they pulled the larger boat to shore. Soon it was tied to the dock in the deserted park, and they were back to the business of the tour.

"Let's try again," Arnie said, pointing his boat out into the waves. We'll see what the hoi polloi is doing today." They headed toward the south shore.

After a few moments Petrie asked, "When do you think they'll find the body?"

"What body?"

"The body of the guy who fell off that boat."

"Don't be making up stories now," Arnie said.

"I bet he jumped. There's a lot of pressure on these fast-laners, you know. The way the DOW has been nosediving—life isn't easy for them. Their burden is great," Petrie went on, wrinkling his brow with his John Wayne look, "what with the poor economy. Why, it takes a lot of worry and work to manage those investments. All that money to protect and

6

watch. Sure, he ended his misery right here on this beautiful lake. What better place? Death on a quiet Monday morning. See how lucky we are? No money to worry about, no fancy sailboats to maintain. *Nada*."

"Hey, cut it out," Arnie laughed.

"Okay, okay, maybe that wasn't it." Petrie paused a moment still thinking, then said, "It must have been his wife. She finally left with his business partner. He knew they've been having an affair for years. Yesterday he caught them in the boathouse—heartbroken, he ended it with a neat dive off the bow—" as he spoke he made a smooth curving motion with his arm, simulating the dive.

"That's enough," Arnie shouted over the motor's quiet roar.

They both laughed and settled back to enjoy the ride. The wind was gusty and waves splashed them as they moved along. Soon they reached the protection of the south shoreline and cruised it, going counter-clockwise in the quiet edge of water, out of the wind. They glided past yard after yard, the little motor humming contentedly.

Even though both men were familiar with the lake, they were always struck by the size of the houses, the huge calendar-picture lawns, often shaded by stately oaks and maples. Each house had its obligatory private dock, reaching out into the water like a wooden finger, pointing in unison with the others, to the center of the lake as if something note-worthy abounded there.

Always present were the boats: the ubiquitous pontoon, the sleek sailboat, the large runabout, and on shore, the occasional upturned canoe.

"Look at this one," Petrie said, breaking the temple-like silence, pointing to a house with a ridiculously large window facing the water. "That window is as wide as my entire house."

"I'll take the one next to it," Arnie quipped. "Now that's a house for a king." It was a large three-story mansion of lannon stone, with a great patio and guest house to match. "That carriage house is bigger than my bungalow."

"That tells you who you are," Petrie declared. "Look there," he pointed. "An airplane! Two cars—one, two, three, four boats, and an airplane! That guy travels on land, water, and in the air!" A red pontoon plane sat smartly pulled up beside a large dock before a rambling brick house that seemed to go on forever. "What next?" he concluded.

More surprises met the men as they slipped along the shoreline. The ostentatious display that littered the yards and rested dockside soon brought no further verbal response. They grew silent, as if numbed.

Then they found the eastern shore, still out of the wind, and still silently observing the glitter of the water and the wealth.

Petrie acknowledged, again, that it was a beautiful day. Tired of the shoreline, he studied the lake, its body dotted with gently rolling white caps at play in the early fall wind. *A sacred day*, he thought. *Everyone else is at work and here we are, stealing it from them.*

A hint of guilt came over him—as if he and his friend were swiping a few golden moments away from the world of work. Glancing at Arnie, he noticed a gaze that seemed to indicate similar thoughts. No other humans were on the water; only these two men, dressed in faded sweat shirts and pants, wearing sweat-lined lightweight baseball caps advertising snowmobiles and Toyotas.

The world has left us behind, Petrie mused to himself. For an instant he felt ignored, neglected, as if he and his companion did not work hard enough, did not do enough for society, and had been banished, set adrift on the open sea.

Then, coming around a point of land jutting out into the water, the men suddenly were confronted with an isolated cove filled with rows of sailboats that in their owners' attempts to be just a little different, were nonetheless, all the same. Each had a name painted proudly onto the stern that shouted cleverness. The boats were secured in individual slips beside three large wooden docks.

"The Yacht Club," Arnie said more to himself than to his friend, breaking the silence.

The huge dockside clubhouse glistened in the sunshine, its white paint contrasting with the blue sky and water. An oversized American flag fluttered proudly on a tall white pole growing out of its roof. A second flag flew below it wearing the logo of the club: a blue sailboat on a clean white background. On the far end of the dock nearest to them stood a small bright sign, stark in its isolation, that discreetly but firmly said one word: PRIVATE.

"Private, private, private," muttered Petrie, shaking his head. "Is that the only word these people know—their mantra? Let's go in and have a drink."

"They wouldn't serve us," replied Arnie. "We haven't made it yet."

"Yet?" countered Petrie. "You mean we're trying to make it?"

Arnie turned the old Amundson boat north, away from the club, as Petrie snapped a sharp salute to the flags, then another to the smaller sign.

"There's not much to see on the north shore except railroad tracks. How about a lecture on railroading, Arnie? Tell me about how the railroad barons built the Midwest. Tell me what they thought of those sacred white bears that live down by this lake."

"Go to hell—I'm heading this thing back home. We've been out here for over an hour. That's enough. I've got some Old Milwaukee in the frig—we can sit on the back porch and finish it off."

Coming around the last point in the lake, the men suddenly noticed a flashing red light at the public dock. Still too far away to make it all out, Petrie remarked, "You see—I was right. They found the body."

They were now in rougher water, cutting against the wind, the waves sometimes splashing into the boat. "Let's head over there and see what's up," Arnie said.

After several minutes they arrived at the park and tied up near the sailboat. Stepping onto the dock Petrie asked the county sheriff standing beside the boat what had happened.

"It looks like a suicide. The old fellow from the gas station. He went out to test this little outboard this morning and didn't come back. He must be out there somewhere. We're going to have to drag for him."

❧ 2 ❧

Denny's Declaration

We are all convention; convention carries us away,
and we neglect the substance of things.

—Montaigne, 1580

IT WAS FOUR O'CLOCK in the afternoon. The early spring sun stayed in the western sky a few seconds longer than the day before, throwing a welcome pale light over the two-storied brick building that stood with several like it along the downtown block of the small suburban town.

Denny sat in the chair, his legs out and crossed, his chin in the palm of his right hand, his elbow braced on the chair's arm. It was a small shop, unlike those multi-chaired chains that appeared throughout the country in the last decade. The red, white and blue electrically operated barber pole still hung outside, still spiraled the patriotic colors, spinning them around again and again. It had faded in the years of hot summer sunlight, but it was still there, turning each day—spinning like the earth—each day the shop was open. Denny had only one chair, a large old black-leathered monster with cast-iron frame. It was a giant relic of

10

the past, yet it worked well. It had a hydraulic lift that he operated by a lever on its side. If he wanted to raise the chair he simply pumped the lever a bit. To lower it he engaged a foot pedal at the chair's base.

He sometimes thought of how the town's men put themselves into his hands. He could elevate or lower them at will. And with a few ill-directed passes of the sharp shears or electric clipper, he could devastate them. And the razor! How they trusted him with it! How many necks had he shaved? How much blood coursed through veins only a tiny fraction of an inch from the edge of that sharp blade?

But, today his eyelids began to close as his head fell. The usual customers had come by, their clipped hair lying in a heap by the push broom beside the wall at the shop's back door. After each haircut he swept the trimmings into that pile and in a busy day the different colors mixed. Only at the end of the day did he bend to sweep it into the dustpan, and then let it slide into the white plastic-lined wastebasket. That basket was one place that the town's people got along, he thought, one place where they mixed intimately.

He knew there were other such places, resting places of sorts, like the two cemeteries where they finally came together, and the sewers even, where their waste intermingled. And then there was Denny's compost pile at the rear of his small lot where the hair turned into a dark loam as it decomposed with the yard's shredded leaves. He used hair as fertilizer, used it to help grow his onions, tomatoes, lettuce, and the few rows of red potatoes he cultivated each season. This frugality, he often thought, must have come from his hardworking Germanic ancestors.

The gardening was a little legacy he enjoyed. It took him back to the rural Minnesota farm of his youth, that place in his memory he cherished more and more with the passing years. Gardens were part of that world.

These were his thoughts this afternoon. That life back then, out on the land had come to an end, and he knew his days in the shop were also numbered. Now in his late sixties, he felt the years of labor, felt the years of shallow verbal interchanges with the town's affluent menfolk.

His brow suddenly furrowed as he concluded it was time to leave, move to Arizona maybe, if Yvonne would consent to go. She professed to love this town, this suburb they'd called home for almost forty years. Besides, she liked to remind him, the kids lived nearby with the grandchildren. How could she ever move so far away from all that love?

Denny studied the sun, partially hidden by black oak trees that stood behind the buildings across the street. The lingering afternoon light was becoming brighter with each day. Those oak branches were busy, invisibly drawing sap up to their smallest twigs where the still-tight buds waited with their spring thirst.

In the distance, just past the corner of the post office, he could see a portion of the frozen lake several blocks away. The sun's warmth was working to transform its ice. It was a big lake, good for fishing, although in the past several years it had given over to pleasure craft, more and more sailboats and those colorfully dressed water skiers from the city. They came in increasing numbers on the weekends. The popular loud jet skis puzzled Denny. He wondered what the attraction was, speeding over the surface of the water in those little things, not trying to get anywhere, just going, just moving fast.

In his honesty, Denny admitted he saw fewer and fewer people fishing each year. Maybe it was true what those environmentalists were saying about the lake's water, that its purity was a thing of the past. Maybe the fisher folk were driving further out for their recreation.

He watched the changes from his shop window for years. And the changes were not just going on outside the shop, for things had become different inside as well. Fewer and fewer youngsters, fewer families were using his haircutting services. More and more it was the professionals, the businessmen. No women had recently ventured in for a trim, none he could recall. They must be using the many hair salons that were found today in the strip malls that ringed the town. Fashion. The salons were fashionable places. He doubted he would know how to trim a woman anyway—all those fancy hairdos. His training had not included cutting a woman's hair.

Barber college seemed like something belonging to ancient history. How many years has it been? For years upon years, he had clipped the hair of the town's menfolk. Hair styles changed; the men changed. Yes, more and more, his clientele was the upscaled professional. The upwardly mobile. These men said little of substance to Denny, sometimes seemed not to see him.

Yet, it had been a good income, although minimal, compared to that of most of his customers. He paid off the mortgage two years before, and Yvonne was pleased about that.

"Now," she said, "we are going to save for a trip to Mexico. Cancun or Cozumel. Susan and Jack went last year and loved it. All these years I have not asked for much, but now I want to go."

Mexico, Schmexico, Denny responded to himself. He thought again of the black oak branches across the street. They formed a latticework that filtered and diverted the sun's rays, so they came to his shop from different angles. Over the years those oak trees had grown, Denny realized. All that growth in one spot. Those trees have never gone to Mexico, nor had they mortgages to pay.

His reverie was broken by a hunter-green SUV as it turned the corner by the post office and parked across the street. Two men had apparently left their offices early and driven home to get haircuts before the shop closed.

"Hey, Den," one said as he entered.

"Hello, Denny," followed the other.

They hung their coats on the pole by the door as Denny rose and readied his white cotton bib. One settled into the ancient barber chair as the other took a seat by the window and reached for a *Field and Stream*.

"What's up, Den?" one asked as the cape was fastened around his neck and draped over his shoulders and lap.

"Not much. Not much today. Quiet—it's been quiet."

"How about it, Den? Is it going to be early or late this year? Most of the snow is gone already."

"Too soon to tell. Too soon. We need a few warm nights to really get it started. It'll be a while yet," Denny replied as his eyes rose to the portion of the lake visible through the window.

Each spring for years and years it was he who announced when the ice went out. Some years the local shopkeepers held contests to see who could guess when this event would occur. Certificates for free merchandise were given to the few who came closest. Other years, though, there was no hoopla. At those times, Denny just added another date onto the chart on the shop's wall. Yellow-lined school paper. Simple. Just the fact of the melted ice. The fact of open water.

The two customers started to talk to each other as Denny went about his work. The gentle sound of his sharp scissors was a backdrop to their conversation. The cozy, warm smell of talcum powder joined the mix.

"Japan. That's our next trip," one said. "We'll be there for at least seven or eight days—and the workshop should take another three or four. I'm going over the specs now."

"That's the first part of May, isn't it?" asked the one with the magazine. "When I was in Tokyo last fall it was beautiful."

"Ya—May seventh. George says we may be going to Sweden after that. There's a group over there that wants to see how our software will adapt to a new urban heating project. It should be a big deal."

Denny listened. This was the way it often was. Business. Travel. Work and wealth. His haircuts traveled far. They flew first class on Delta, American, Northwest, and many more. Would you care for champagne?

He smelled the men's cologne, saw the dirt in their ears, found the early signs of baldness, the gray hairs. He dusted them with talcum, laid on a white sheen. He tipped his head to better guide the progress of his sharp shears.

In about thirty minutes, the haircuts were finished. The men paid Denny, one giving him a dollar tip, then both bid farewell as they left the shop. They drove to the country club east of town for a drink before going home. Denny had one more haircut before five and then swept up, slipped into his aging mackinaw with the hood, locked the front door, turned the OPEN/CLOSED sign that hung in the door's window around, flipped off the barber pole switch, and walked to the back door. He snapped off the lights and stepped down into the alley. As he turned to lock the door, he saw it was getting noticeably darker now. He thought of the supper Yvonne would have prepared.

The walk home provided some invigoration. The late afternoon air was cool and served to freshen him, as much as he could be freshened after another week of work. It was only five blocks—the walk. Never, in all these years had Denny driven to the shop. This was one of the appeals to the work, one of the small rewards, he kept telling himself.

He knew the daily walks were good for him. In all sorts of weather, he refused to drive, even in the worst rain, wind, and snow. Neighbors marveled at it. One remarked once, how Denny's regular morning and evening walks were like a Norman Rockwell painting. Here, in the midst of this fast-paced suburb was this barber who bent against the wind, who wore a knitted stocking cap in winter, and wrapped a heavy muffler around his neck in the snow and cold, and who firmly held a sturdy black umbrella against the rain—but who stayed with it, who walked each day.

Today he maneuvered the five blocks quickly, perhaps driven on by his hunger. Turning in at the blacktop driveway, he soon was at the side door, where the green newspaper tube that was affixed to the side of the house held its open mouth tipped up as if it was a large-mouth bass reaching for a frog. Normally it would have held the evening paper, but last fall the evening paper ended. None was published in the entire metro area anymore. Both dailies went to a morning edition and the fat, ad-laden Sunday paper that was published early on Saturdays. That Sunday paper always held "news" that was a full-day old. Now the daily paper, delivered at dawn by an anonymous adult, came in a plastic bag tossed upon the front steps. And like its heavy Sunday cousin, it brought yesterday's news. Denny felt there was not much purpose in reading it. He learned the news the night before on the late TV news show.

Denny was determined not to take the tube down. He left it as a reminder of another time, of the time of the evening paper. For years it had been, like his determined walks, another of his quiet, private pleasures—relaxing in his stuffed chair with the newspaper after a day's work. But that was history now.

Immediately upon opening the door he smelled the familiar aroma of fried potatoes and onions. This time the welcome old smell was joined by the meaty scent of what turned out to be fried pork steak. Yvonne showed her age by her cooking, refusing to switch to the trendy pasta and stir-fried dinners that leapt out at her from the colorful photos in the paper's weekly food section. Fried potatoes were often on the breakfast menu and again at night. Yvonne too, quietly held her ground, refusing to change what was dear to her.

THE NEXT WEEK'S WEATHER was unseasonably warm, so Denny decided he had better keep a close watch on the ice. On Wednesday a large patch opened up in the middle of the lake. Then Thursday morning, he saw that the entire western shore was open. The night's wind moved most of the remaining pack to the east shore with its numerous small coves. He knew as he opened the shop that morning that he would have to keep a vigil throughout the day. The ice could be gone in a day or two.

His procedure was to determine, as best he could, when the entire shoreline was free of ice, at least when a boat could be put into the water from any place along the shore. The last of the ice was often pushed over to the eastern end, due to the prevailing west winds.

So, Thursday afternoon after closing the shop, he hurried home. Yvonne knew what to expect, so she held dinner, knowing Denny would back the Chevrolet from the garage to circle the lake, inspecting the shoreline.

Immediately upon turning onto Lake Drive, he spotted the white color of the remaining ice pack way over in the far southeast corner, in Simper's Cove. It held all that was left of the winter's ice, and Denny felt it would disappear sometime through the night. Certain it was still hours before the final meltdown, he drove the car home.

After supper, the rains started. Finally, after the ten p.m. news, Denny felt he had better have a look. Taking his mackinaw, his flat wool Scotsmen's cap, the sturdy umbrella, a flashlight, and feeling his side pocket to be sure his pocket watch was with him, he climbed into the Chevrolet and drove off.

At Simper's Cove, he parked on the street and walked up to a three-storied stone house to ring the bell. As was often the case, he had to walk on private property to check the ice, and he felt he had better get permission. This time the late hour caused some delay but finally the back porch light went on and the door opened a crack. Denny explained to the middle-aged gentlemen what his purpose was—that he wanted permission to walk on his property down to the lake to inspect the melting of the ice.

Simper's Cove, unfortunately for Denny, had no developed public access, and its far shore was not visible from anywhere else on the public shoreline. The only other way to view it was from the water, and Denny had never had to use a boat for his work. The citizens knew of his annual endeavor and generally cooperated. They let him walk their lawns to the lake to observe, to mark the time the ice went out. However, tonight it was different. The man at the door stared at Denny with a puzzled look.

"I'd like to walk down to your lake shore to check the ice," Denny said. "To note just when it melts."

As he finished, Denny understood the man's hesitation. This was one of the new houses, one of the large three-storied showplaces to appear on the lakeshore during the past year or two. This man was a stranger, a recent resident to the town.

"What?" was his reply.

Denny patiently explained his intent again and added that he did this each spring—that it was a tradition of sorts.

"No. It's late for God's sake. It's after eleven," the man said as he started to close the door.

Surprised, Denny tried to explain again. "I do this each spring. It'll only take a moment. I've done it for years."

"What for?" the man asked, raising his brow for emphasis. "What's the sense of it? No, it's too late."

With that he closed the door. Denny heard the deadbolt click. He stood, momentarily stunned. Never before had he been refused permission to walk beside someone's house, to tread on their lawn on his way to view the lake. Hurriedly he returned to his car, started to drive slowly down the street as he bent forward to look at the other houses, hoping to recognize one whose owner he knew. He realized he was in a row of four or five of the new upscaled, oversized houses.

He thought he would turn around and try the other side of the cove. It was all that was left to him, his only option, but he knew that this past summer and fall workers had been busy on its shoreline as well. Smaller houses were bought up, torn down, and new bigger ones erected. All of Simper's Cove shoreline had been upscaled, he feared.

There was only one hope. That was the stretch of slough on that side of the cove, the weedy drainage ditch that was the water's outlet on this side of the lake. He decided to take a look, perhaps to try to walk along its narrow edge, at least far enough for a glimpse of the lake, far enough to determine if the ice had gone.

So it came to that. Denny parked the car beside the road where the ditch lay between two new houses. It was a neglected part of the shoreline, unable to be developed. Now filled head-high with last year's brown cattails, it presented a difficult terrain. Luckily, Denny had prepared by slipping on his tall rubber boots, but even they were not really adequate. The slough ice had melted and the underlying mud was getting soft with the lengthening days, and Denny sunk in at times, nearly up to his knees.

But the distance was not far, less than half a block or so, and Denny was determined. He struggled along, sometimes pushing the still standing dead foliage aside as he slowly advanced. Finally arriving at the shoreline, both feet cold from the icy water, he stepped out onto the beach and saw the last of the icepack. Not needing a flashlight, he studied it as it lay pushed up onto the sand. There was hardly any of the crumbled ice left, the rains having done a good job of melting it, and together with the day's persistent, prevailing west wind, it was only a matter of time. It would be entirely gone within the hour, in fact, Denny concluded; it was really all finished now.

He used his flashlight to check his pocket watch. "Eleven thirty-seven p.m.," he declared to himself. "This year it's eleven thirty-seven p.m."

ଛ 3 ଓ

Cookie Day

Our passions debase us. Our
needs make fools of us all.

—Michael Perry, 2005

OHN TISCHENDORF WALKED SLOWLY from the faculty parking lot toward his office in Goldstein Hall. His tall, thin figure was covered by a long, heavy, gray winter overcoat, buttoned at the chin. His shoulders were thrown back as if he was trying to rid himself of an unwanted weight, and the cool December air filled his lungs as he purposely took deep, measured breaths, forcing fresh blood—he imagined—to surge through his veins. His night had been nearly sleepless.

The cold reminded him that it was winter solstice time, a few days when night was as long as it would get, when the world was in a cosmic balancing act. The Ancients were never sure which way the earth would lean—toward lengthening daylight or ever increasing darkness. Uncertain if spring would ever come back, if the never-ending struggle between light and dark would tip toward one or the other, they watched each day anxiously. Ceremonies had to be affected, rituals carried out to help assure the end of another winter—to help bring the sunlight.

But this seasonal musing—lecture hall in nature—was pulling him away from a more immediate concern. "Would she drive in today," he asked himself, desiring to be with her, to seek forgiveness and to see her smile the way she had in the past, when, their problem overcome, they moved on to other things.

After several months together, she had left. They both felt that marriage was a possibility, but there were still so many things she wanted to accomplish: to get back to Europe for a season . . . and that Ph.D. She was determined to complete the coursework and get the dissertation started. These were priorities. This morning he felt that he had been unkind, accusing her of undue assertiveness and of trying to alter his routine.

It was early, only a little after seven. The morning darkness was just giving way. One other car sat in the parking lot, a lone set of footprints between it and the administration building nestling in the tall frosted pines that highlighted this part of the campus. It was as if the car was anchored to the brick building by the footprint-chain that lay on the clean white blanket of snow that fell the night before. The walker, apparently unprepared for the first snowfall, had still worn waffle-soled running shoes, and the little black squares of the imprints were like windows through which the asphalt gasped for breath. Waffle windows, too small to let enough air in, thought Tishendorf, as he breathed deeply, trying to rid his chest of its constriction.

The snow was less than an inch thick, but heavy and wet, covering everything. The heat of the asphalt, from the unseasonably warm weather, had, like their romance, lingered into mid-December. It quickly melted the thin snow pressed down by the walker.

"It must be terrible to be smothered," Tishendorf thought as he left the parking lot, and stepped onto the concrete sidewalk that curved around the pines, leading to Goldstein Hall. *Smothering—an interesting word. S-mothering—to be engulfed, suffocated by a female? To smother some-*

thing is to cover it, to contain it, to the terminal point of existence, he thought, lecturing to himself.

"Come off it, Tish," he concluded. "Enjoy this day—this start of the holidays. Today is the last day of classes. This afternoon Christmas vacation begins. Enjoy it and don't think about her."

Upon reaching Goldstein, he stamped his feet as he pulled the heavy door open, then quickly stepped inside. A wall of sickly warm air hit him. *Doesn't someone turn the thermostat down at night?* he thought irritably. *This building is so energy efficient that nothing leaks out nor in! Nothing gives. Nothing bends even a little bit. How lucky those people are who teach in older buildings with creaky wooden floors, drafty rooms, and windows that can be thrown open at will.* For Professor Tishendorf, one of life's greatest little pleasures was to stand in an overly heated classroom before an open window on a winter's day, arms akimbo, breathing in the cold outside air.

Reaching to unbutton his overcoat and pulling off his scarf, Tischendorf's eyes automatically went to the bronze bust of Abraham P. Goldstein standing on its pedestal in the foyer facing the doorway. He was the benefactor who gave the money needed to construct the building over thirty years ago. John nodded his head and muttered, "Good morning Abraham," as he had done for years each morning. He always felt a bit sorry for old Goldstein, looking out over the parking lot with that hollow gaze in his bronze eyes. No one really knew who Abraham was anymore, or seemed to care. In fact he was downright neglected, especially at this time of year. Each December he had to share his foyer with a lavishly decorated fir tree, which stood beside him, covered with all sorts of trinkets, that members of the support staff devotedly hung on its boughs.

"Fir trees are phallic," John recalled hearing himself say in a classroom the week before. "They're embedded in mother earth, like obelisks and tapered candles, all standing at attention." This caused a titter of amusement to run through his student audience. This morning John paused for a moment, looking at the tree, testing the statement he had made in the class. *Why sure*, he thought, *that's why they can't wait to decorate it, to adorn it with their little plastic angels, lambs, and red and green balls. To them, a tree with its roots cut off—a dead tree—means life. Freud must have loved the European custom of cutting a tall, pointed conifer and, after bringing it into the warm, safe enclosure of a room, to see it lovingly trimmed and finally to have an exploding star placed at its tip! Reproduction! Yes, Christmas, like many human sacred ceremonies, is speaking to that species-wide desire to survive. We're always celebrating it.* Then, after a moment of simply staring at the tree without any thought, he suddenly told himself, *Oh, hell—get off it! What do you really know?*

His condescending soliloquy embarrassed him, and glad it was finished, he turned to move down the hallway toward the stairs leading to his office on the third floor. Heading toward him was one of the building's custodians, Jesse Mashefski, with his short rotund body, topped by a glistening dome.

"Good morning, John. Merry Christmas."

"Hi, Jesse."

"How d'ya like the white stuff?"

"Ya, great."

"Temp's supposed ta drop this afternoon. Cold front movin' in. Better dig out the electric blanket, John."

"Okay, Jesse," Tischendorf replied, forcing a smile over his shoulder as he turned to climb the stairs. "See you later."

Yes, he's right, thought Tischendorf. *I needed that blanket last night. I hope it's not a long, cold winter.*

Reaching the second floor, he paused an instant before climbing to the third. Then, he turned and walked down the corridor to the stairs at the other end. On his right was the front office of the Psychology Department, still unlit. The secretary wouldn't be in before eight. Then came the doors to the faculty offices on both sides: Pete Wittgenstein, Sally Wilson, Phil Cepak, and then the last office, its plastic name plate saying, Marie M. Masterman. *Good morning, Marie*, he said to himself as he passed. *Did you sleep well last night? Your leaving is best for us isn't it?*

Now you can go on to those projects, and I am free again. When will you be by to pick up your things?

He finally climbed to the third floor and the Sociology Department. Flipping on the light in the outer office and checking his mail, he found a red-and-green flyer saying:

Cookie Day!!
Come—Eat Cookies—Be Merry
Friday: 10:00-3:00
Goldstein Conference Room

Cookie Day. He had forgotten it. Each year on the last day of classes before Christmas, the secretaries put on a sugar-fest for the staff in Goldstein. Tossing the flyer into the recycling tub, he left the mailroom and continued on down the hall to his office.

His eight o'clock lecture on social stratification went as it had for years. Most students, all twenty-three who showed up, were sleepy and uninterested. But the three senior sociology majors seemed aware of his preoccupation. (He wondered if they heard of his break-up.) The lecture hall was on the first floor of Goldstein with only a partial view of the parking lot. Casting the requisite instructor-student eye contact aside, he scanned the lot off and on for the entire fifty minutes. *Was that her red Honda? No, Marie never came to school this early. She has classes today—would she cut them?*

As he lectured, Tischendorf listened to himself. He liked to do that—listen to himself while discussing something. It was as though he were two people. This morning he marveled at his ability to lecture on Marx's thesis of class struggle while at the same time watching for the small red car. At last the bells rang, the students shuffled out, and he climbed the steps back to the office.

Right at ten o'clock, Joan Kirkpatrick, the department secretary, was at his open door. "Be sure to go down for Cookie Day. Don't wait too long. The best go fast."

"Thanks, Joan," Tichendorf replied, turning away from his computer. "I'll be right down."

Later, as he entered the conference room, he was instantly reminded of the scene acted out here each year at this time. Cookie Day was an institution. Sugar was everywhere. Frosting, nectar—all forms and colors of sweets competed with the thick, dark aroma of freshly brewed coffee. Someone had drawn the dark, plush drapes, leaving the room in a subdued light from the several candles sitting on the banquet table. A hidden tape player was subtly issuing quiet Christmas music.

Going to the table, decorated with silky red and green clothes, white yule logs with candles, and little holly wreaths, Tichendorf took an offered plate and began to fill it with the rich food. He started with dark, moist brownies, covered with white powdered sugar. Then came the creamed chocolate balls, large as marble shooters, laced with a generous amount of brandy. Chocolate cakes were everywhere—sheet cakes, layered cakes, some with two, three, four layers, and even one with six. He took a piece of the latter and found that maraschino cherries lay hidden between its thin layers. Then came the cookies: peanut butter with chocolate kisses pushed down into them, all shapes of flat, light sugar cookies: green stars, bells and red Santa's climbing into chimneys. His plate was filled, and he had only begun to move along the large table. The entire section of the light, flaky Scandinavian pastries beckoned to him, but he could not respond. He turned away, took the cup of coffee offered by a willing hand, and looked for an empty chair. The room was becoming busy as more and more people strolled in.

He found a seat, sipped the coffee and scanned the room for Marie, then remembered she had a class until eleven thirty on Fridays. Then his stomach began to tell him of the rich food: sugar, chocolate, and coffee. Even the air was thick with a sweet, syrupy perfume.

Clearing his plate, he was chided by someone to go again, to get more. And he did, this time loading up on the Swedish pastries, especially the rosettes that he loved. Finally sated, he sat back in the chair, sipping his coffee. People were standing in small groups of two and three, holding plates of sweets, chatting and trying to sip coffee all at the same time. Others were seated in the plush conference chairs, talking in subdued voices, captured by the tenor of the room. It was almost silent, yet filled with activity.

Turning inward again, John asked, *What is this? What is this Cookie Day? We don't need these sweets. What did the ancients do without sugar? How were they seduced? They survived. Why do we moderns coat ourselves inside and out with it?* Then the room became darker, its syrupy walls crowded around him as his breathing momentarily faltered. Rising quickly, he dropped his paper plate, Styrofoam cup, and red paper napkin into the wastebasket and slipped out into the corridor. He hurried up to his office.

The conference room scene was loud in his imagination as he stood before his office window looking down on the now nearly filled parking lot. He thought of the early custom of the Arctic Inuit in which men spent days and nights in their own snow house, telling boasting stories, arm wrestling, cajoling, entreating their allies to laugh, to party. In a world without the intoxicating effects of alcohol, in the early times, they ate food brought to them by the women, container after sealskin container of food, for days and days. Like the early Romans with their vomitoria, the Inuit men would periodically exit the snow house to stand in the winter darkness to regurgitate, to expel the swallowed food so more could be consumed.

And what about us—this orgy of sweets! Tischendorf asked himself. *Why do we do this? Is it really the solstice? Do we fall into a feeding frenzy in this time when the earth stands still? How foolish. Don't we know it's winter, and the worst is yet to come? We should be preparing for the cold and ice of January. Why all this laughing, dancing in the dark face of danger, of death?*

Now nearly noon, the parking lot was busy with students, many leaving campus for daytime jobs. Looking down, he saw them sometimes shouting at each other, waving, even running to their automobiles. They were like children, filled with the present, pleased with the start of vacation.

Not wanting lunch, Tischendorf stayed in his office, going over materials for his one-o'clock class. It was Social Psychology, and his favorite by far. This term's students were among his best in a few years, able and willing to engage. Today they were to discuss dramaturgy—how social interaction was akin to a theatrical performance, complete with a script and scenic props. He enjoyed raising the question of agency, of what made it all work. He knew already, as he glanced at the darkened computer monitor at his side, that he'd discuss Cookie Day, bring it up, and let this group of young minds run with it. He would ask them to think about the seductive conference room and how the ideas of Cooley and Mead could be used for an interpretation.

But, while the intellectual interaction was inviting, today was all too much for him. He was invigorated, pulled along by the demands of his work, but the previous night weighed heavily. He was exhausted and wanted the day to come to a close. This next class was his last. He wished it were over.

Brought back by the sudden ring of his telephone, he picked it up, said simply, "John Tischendorf," and was met with Marie's voice. "John," she started, "let's do dinner tonight. I need to come over for my stereo and the few bathroom things, anyway. We could cook. What do you think?"

And so it was arranged. He could not chat further since it was already one o'clock, and he was late for class. Grabbing his textbook and folder of notes, he hurried to the lecture hall.

It was two-thirty when he pushed away from the desk and knew his day was done. His stomach and the pulsating veins around his temples told him the sugar and chocolate were hard at work. Rising, he reached behind his door, found the heavy winter coat and in an instant was moving down the stairs. Passing Abraham Goldstein, he said aloud, "Happy Holidays, Abe. You take care of yourself. See you in January."

The afternoon skies had cleared and the sun was making quick work of last night's snow, but Tischendorf was, nevertheless, not fooled. He knew the depths of winter still lay ahead. There would be much more snow, ice, and darkness. He moved slowly along the curving concrete walkway through the fir trees and soon stepped onto the wet asphalt. This day's length would be the same as tomorrow's he knew, and maybe even the next, but then the days would grow longer. Slowly the time of light would increase, and spring would come again as it had from the beginning.

❧ 4 ☙

Three Suburban Pieces

It's good to be reminded that each
of us has a different dream.

—Richard Nelson, 1989

1.
Red Bird's Lament

HE TWO MEN SAT in the yellow-green plastic and aluminum lawn chairs. Their gazes lazily fixed on the empty neighborhood street in front of the house.

"Paradise," one said. "We live in paradise."

The other replied by contemplatively raising his eyebrows and nodding. "Yes," he said, "and to think I almost agreed to that transfer three years ago. Couldn't you see Lynn and me with the kids sweating it out in Houston, trying to keep our lawn green?"

The two friends understood each other. Their conversation that late May afternoon droned on like the traffic that filled Highway 53, two blocks away. Coming and going, going and coming. The SUVs, muscle cars, minivans, and crew-cab pickups moved unceasingly, the sounds of their engines only slightly buffered by the Colorado blue spruces marking the back lot line.

"Perfect," the older, balding one said again. "It's a perfect day." The men were sitting in the dappled shade of a diseased elm tree that canopied the backyard. It's new leaves were a mixture of green, yellow, and brown. The old elm had withstood the dreaded beetle for years but finally was being overtaken. It was only a matter of time.

"Why the lawn food? We really don't need it here in Lake Superior Country, do we?"

"Hey—it won't hurt. They say you should give your lawn a boost early in spring."

"Where d'ja get it?"

"Home Depot. On sale. Two ninety-nine a bag. Doesn't it smell good?"

A sprinkler was at work beside the house. A row of small streams of fluoridated water rose twenty feet into the air, lazily arched, hesitated for an instant, before falling with increasing speed to the earth. It dissolved the tiny chartreuse granules of lawn food, washed them down to the roots of the grass.

The pungent smell of the fertilizer drifted to the backyard. Back and forth, back and forth, the sheet of water moved. A plastic, marble-like dark-green birdbath held by two nymph figures stood in a bed of budding peony bushes and was being drenched as well. The water loosened the winter grime that had settled on the statues, cleansing them, bringing back their original vitality.

"Wal-Mart had it for two seventy-nine. I was there this morning pricing the flowering crabs."

"Still too high. It's been going up for years. I see where Brazil is starting to export the stuff. That should be cheaper."

As the afternoon wore on, the dying elm's shadows darkened, and the skin of the men's faces and bare arms assumed a mottled greenish-yellow tone. Their speech became punctuated with longer stretches of silence as they drank beer, dreamily smoked cigarettes, and let the sounds, smells, and colors of the day drift over them.

The beer slowed their minds.

The orange tabby cat that lived with the balding man and his family rose from its nap in the sunshine on the porch, stretched, then sat for a moment on the top step. He was a scarred veteran of many love battles and two years ago, his life changed. That encounter left him with a single eye, the other removed by the young vet up at the shopping center on the highway, who took one look and said, "Let me neuter him. That will end the fighting." It was done. Now he rarely left the yard.

The cat watched the sheet of water sweep over the lawn, back and forth. Sparrows drawn to the yard by the sprinkler fluttered in the mountain ash beside the asphalt drive. A lone starling suddenly appeared and landed under the falling drops. It walked as bold as a biped, enjoying the bath on the wet grass. A pair of cardinals, more hesitant, kept their distance at the top of the ash tree. The male's bright coat was a patch of red cloth caught in the branches. The buff-colored female perched below him, to the left.

The cat's eye locked onto the parading starling, and he began to creep down the steps to the cover of the peony bushes, but the bird spied him and bolted from the yard. Undaunted, the cat took a position under the yews at the driveway's edge just outside the reach of the water. He waited for new prey. The men saw him.

"I still think the trade stinks."

"No-no, it was a good one. An over-the-hill pitcher with a tired arm for a power hitter who'll hit twenty-five home runs?" the bald man said.

"Not in the dome. Maybe outside with a helping wind, but not in that dead air. The ball doesn't carry inside that dome."

The green men watched as the scarlet bird suddenly glided to the birdbath and began to enjoy the water. Wings drenched, it dropped to the ground and was instantly pounced upon by the cat. The female flew down from her perch, dove at the cat, then returned to the tree and was

31

silent. There was no call, no cry. The droning traffic continued as the water rose and fell, back and forth, back and forth. Holding the struggling bird to the ground with his mouth and forepaws, the cat's single eye wide open, the cat made two quick bites to ensure death. After raising his head to scan the yard, he turned the bird over with a front paw then gripped it tightly with his jaws, lifted it from the wet grass and stepped smartly through the falling water to the cement walk that ran beside the house to the back lot.

The men's marble-like eyes followed the red and orange colors moving along the sidewalk.

"I like the dome. They say domes are old fashioned, but I like it. Those cities tearing them down to build open-air stadiums will be sorry. Rain or shine the game goes on."

"Ya, that's right. And with the new style artificial grass the problems are gone. No more big bounces or turf-burns. It's sure looks natural—just like real grass. No problem of overpriced turf builder there. Maybe we should get that stuff for our yards."

The cat carried the bird, feet up, wings spread, its head swinging like a pendulum with the killer's gait. He mounted the porch steps, placed his prize beside the screen door, and he crouched over it like a lion with a downed gazelle.

"It's been done," one said. "I think it was somewhere down south. Raised hell with the neighbors."

Cold cigarette butts nestled in the gray ashes in an oversized pink ceramic ashtray on the grass beside the empty brown beer bottles. The men did not move as the cat devoured the breast and throat of the red bird. Exhaust from the sport utility vehicles, muscle cars, and minivans reached into the lot and mixed with the smell of the fertilizer.

A woman opened the door, stepped over the ravaged, red-feathered body, moved down the steps and along the walk to the water faucet on the house's side. She turned the water off, returned, and as she climbed the steps, paused to turn to the silent figures and ask, "Can I bring you more beer?"

They sat as if unaware of her presence. She closed the door behind her.

The distant traffic droned on. In the garden the peony nymphs, washed clean by the sprinkled water, came alive with a wet plastic brightness as the female cardinal flew to the top of the dying elm and began to chirp a few brief notes, calling for her mate.

2.
Small Spaces

LAST NIGHT AS I SAT on the cold, wooden bleachers inside our town's small ice arena watching my son's last hockey game of the season, I thought about how tiny the building was. It held the sheet of ice, a small warming room, two smaller dressing rooms, and a berth for the propane-powered, ice-smoothing machine—the Zamboni—and little else. A walkway, eight feet wide, or so, that wrapped around the ice, passed the single set of steel-framed, wooden-benched bleachers. The building was a small concrete shell and little more. Built with public funds, it had a single purpose and did not cost much. Likewise, it did not cost much to maintain. It was a small, cold space, yet it witnessed some heated emotions as hotly contested hockey games were fought there regularly.

We humans need a sense of space. Scholars tell us we could not function without a temporal and spatial awareness. Before me was my son with his teammates, protecting their space, trying to encroach upon—penetrate really—their opponents' given space.

My boy has been playing for ten years, so the scene was a familiar one. As I had done so often, I let my mind move from the action on the ice to the action in the entire small building. There was more than a youthful game unfolding in that gray arena.

We did not fill the bleachers. Our youngsters are too old and have played too many years for us to have the enthusiasm of new hockey parents. We were seasoned watchers. Most players did not have family present at all. Now the boys—there were no girls on either team—usually drive themselves to the games. The scene was unlike that found when the youngest skaters play: the mites, squirts, and pee-wees. Our boys were sixteen. Young men. A few even used tobacco—not allowed on the ice—its bulge evident in their lower lips, when after the game they file out of the dressing room in street shoes, their large hockey bags over their shoulders, a pair of sticks in hand.

Most of the dozen persons who watched were mothers. Fathers apparently had other things to do. One set of grandparents was present and some younger brothers and sisters. A few spectators stood beside the rink's boards, watching through the chainlink fence that is the wall above the boards. Two or three stayed in the more distant warming room and peered through the doorway like bystanders watching a parade from shop windows. One mother sat inside the room reading a newspaper.

Across the ice in the players' boxes, the respective coaches oversaw their charges. Each coach had a younger assistant, and together they stood, one pair in each box, shouting to the boys, and occasionally opening and closing the doors for shift changes. Both pairs of coaches wore the popular high-crowned baseball cap—one size fits all—that had become the choice for year-round headwear, spring, summer, fall, and winter. One coach, a quiet office worker by day, wore a black team jacket matched by black exercise pants. The word "coach" was carefully stitched in shiny orange thread onto his left breast. His younger assistant, who drove a school bus during the day, wore a slippery team jacket with the name of the nearby university in oversized block letters sewn onto its front. Clearly a substitute for the real thing, it was the kind of jacket sold at most department stores and becoming more and more popular.

The opposing team's coach wore army fatigues. He was a reservist who worked at the local armory. His military cap, with its scaled-down sergeant's stripes on the crown and its carefully hand-formed bill, was perched squarely onto his head with a flair of militaristic working-class bravado. This one's assistant, more verbal than most, kept busy pacing in the box, flailing his arms about, pointing emphatically at the players on the ice, shouting instructions and reprimands. His uniform was a dirtied team jacket—a summer softball team—from a local construction firm. On its back were the letters: Wally's Builders—You Name It—We Build It. His trousers were faded jeans, and his baseball cap, worn backwards, advertised a popular brand of precision tool ware.

Sports sociologists say some games are like miniature wars. The teams line up at the boundaries of their territories, guarding their sacred spaces like chessmen, equidistant from each other. The coaches and their assistants stand or pace on the sidelines, like generals and their adjuncts, viewing the battle from distant hilltops. As in wars, the scholars say, games carry their own fascination. I thought of this as I sat on the top plank of the bleachers, my back against the cold cement wall. The few scattered fans sat with me, often chatting amongst themselves, about other things, giving only occasionally their attention to the game.

The chess metaphor stayed with me—pawns, rooks, knights, and bishops—all exhibiting patterned behavior. Only on the ice, the players were not following the rules. Knights moved obliquely, pawns were all over the board—none moved just forward or backward. Rooks moved like bishops, and bishops—those cloaked holy men—were nowhere to be found. And the royal couples, where were they?

Were they hidden in their net chambers behind the goalies, those busy netminders who seemed the guardians of some princess's virginity? Two court overseers—were they the jesters?—in black-and-white striped shirts with plain black trousers streaked in and out among the players, at times blowing shrill whistles, giving a semblance of order to the flow of things. Our warrior-sons moved up and down the ice and occasionally checkmated each other as the puck slid and flew quickly under their guidance. The action was broken at the sound of the jesters' whistles or if the black puck found its resting place—its nest—in the net.

Spectators had witnessed it all before. While the pattern of the game still held some fascination, we were veteran onlookers. Perhaps we really did have other fish to fry. The game was not extremely fast or hard fought. The season had been long and the winter harsh.

Then, suddenly the spell was broken. A misguided body check saw two players fall to the ice and glide along over a blue line. As they fell, one pair of gloved hands began to pummel the other with syncopated punches. Right, left, right, left, in rapid succession. The anger of the young man had broken through. One of the generals and his assistant leaned out of their box and shouted at the sight. Black and white stripes quickly ended the fight.

Surprisingly, I shouted, "Out! Throw him out. Out of the game!" My solitary voice was loud and authoritative. It brought the sleepy spectators to life. A few fathers beside me instantly picked up the call. "Out! Throw him out!" they yelled. The almost empty arena reverberated with the calls. A mother, shocked and angered, seated just below and to my left, turned to confront me, saying coldly, "Why not leave the referee decide that?" She was right, of course. Her calculated and rational response, so typical here in the suburbs, contrasted with my spontaneous outburst. I was embarrassed, for my emotion, but more for my interest in the war, for unlike in earlier years, I did not care which team won the contest. Yet I had yelled.

The player was ejected and the game went on, but now the fans were attentive. The angered mother rallied her few friends and they began to earnestly cheer for their sons. Each pass, each shot or save was followed with loud approval or disappointment. My outburst had pulled them into the game. The small arena, with its smaller crowd was filled with shouting. Now there were two battles, one on the ice and one in the bleachers. Parents shouted at parents, but with their voices turned not toward each other, but instead projected out over the ice. To me, the small space that was the arena had become even smaller. The sleepy fans had awakened. They were constructing new walls. They had become players in a new game, in a smaller space.

My minimal interest in the game shifted even more to the activities of my son. I watched him rather than the game. He pleased me as he took his regular shifts on the ice. How smoothly he powered himself, skillfully working with his teammates. What a wonderful skater he had become! Under his large shoulder pads, behind his shiny black helmet and white rubber coated wire facemask, he was suddenly a man. At his left wing position he was busy backchecking, forechecking and moving the puck up and down. He skated with power when necessary. At times he seemed to be flying.

But my interest waned. My son, a young man now, could take care of himself, could fight his own battles. With a few minutes remaining in the game I rose and walked into the warming room to await the game-ending horn.

When it came, the few parents slowly climbed down from the bleachers and filed into the warming room to await the arrival of their gladiators. Parents from one team ignored those from the other in ways known only to humans. The small space of the little room was now a microcosm of the space out on the ice. The two hockey teams were separated in their respective dressing rooms as the two parent teams were bunched at opposite ends of the warming room as if they were separated by a set of blue lines. Each team stood in a few small groups and chatted quietly amongst itself. Like the hockey game just over, this game would end too. The parents with their sons, would leave their small spaces and move through the doors into others as they made their ways home.

3.
Neutered Pets

IT IS SAID THAT PETS often resemble their keepers. You've seen it—the skinny fellow coming down the street with his greyhound on a leash. The guy's spindly legs match the dog's. And there is that overweight bulldog, its sour face full of wrinkles, and when you sneak a peek at its master, you see how she is the same.

Could it be true? Could we unconsciously keep pets that look like us? And if they look like us, do they behave like us? It seems to follow doesn't it—same form, same function? You know, that high-strung poodle with the high-strung owner? And what about all those Rottweilers? Are their owners as aggressive, ready to fight at the drop of a hat, as the dogs are supposed to be?

Nonsense. Maybe it's all nonsense. Who knows? It's probably not worth the time to think about it. But yesterday when walking the few blocks up to the grocery in the little strip mall, when the small kid from down the street came by on his beat-up bicycle, and nearly clipped me in the process—the ragtag kid whose pants were always torn and dirty, the little guy with the baggy Vikings t-shirt that once was white—when this kid zipped by with his shaggy, dirty mutt running at his side, I saw how similar they were. That kid and his dog not only looked alike, they acted alike. Both were in need of some laundering and both were as free as could be. They could be seen most days, seemingly without a care in the world.

This was on my mind when I came back home yesterday. As I reached our little house, the black neutered cat that lives with us met me at the lot line. He's good that way. He rubbed against my ankle and greeted me with his low, gruff, cat-voice. As I glanced down and greeted him back, I wondered if I resembled him—overweight, gruff, and shedding. What was it about him that appealed to me? He made me think about the shaggy boy and dog again, took me back to my walk.

It's spring, and the walk had been invigorating. The neighborhood, with its small houses and lots, was alive. People were out tidying up after an unusually long and harsh winter. A few pushed lawn mowers, their muffled gasoline engines moaning as they sliced through the juicy green shafts of new grass. And here and there the neighborhood pets were out too. Some sat on front walks, some came out to the sidewalk to sniff at me—the dogs mostly—and some frisked about, jumping at the moving rakes and mowers.

I noticed how similar it all was. Our yards and houses were like each other. Carefully spaced, all the houses stood on an imaginary line set back from the street, mimicking one another. Covered mostly with white vinyl clapboards meant to resemble wood, many might have been built by the same contractor using one set of blueprints with only minor variations. But this was an older, established part of town, not one of the newer sections with its tract houses, and still the similarity was strikingly evident. And the landscaping was homogenous as well. In many cases pyramidal junipers were at the house corners, the creeping yews under the large front windows, the rocks and flowering shrubs purposely set at the driveways by the street.

And usually there was the ubiquitous house pet, often, I supposed, neutered. The pets I saw, like the houses and yards, resembled each other. We Americans pride ourselves in our individuality, but on my walk, all this came crashing down. We looked so similar.

One citizen was carefully painting the wooden picket fence that bordered his entire yard, front and back. It took him a full week of painstaking effort to remove the old paint, leaving the pine boards bare. Now he was covering their nakedness with oily-smelling white paint.

"I do it every four years. They won't last otherwise," he told me.

"Ah, I see," I replied, not wanting to take it any further.

So he covered them up—their attractive grain and natural bearing hidden in a white darkness for four more years. On his face and bare arms paint specks mingled with his sweat. I left him to his work.

In the next block, another citizen used a noisy weed-wacker to tear away the early green shoots entangling themselves with the bottom of his chainlink fence. He was too busy to notice the figure passing on his walk. His work left the silver steel fence, his metal boundary marker, clean and crisp, with its message of ownership. This neighbor was telling us what was his, how far his property ran. His pet, a docile longhaired golden retriever lay on the front steps, out of the way of all the noise and commotion.

We really do clean up in spring. Our landscapes are trimmed, freshened for another summer season. We, I thought, take bearings on our boundaries, marking them anew. Winter's snow, that in some cases obliterates our lot lines, leaves us, and we feel exposed. Our yards lie uncovered for all to see, and the residue of the long winter must be removed. And in some way our pets help with this work.

After greeting each other I picked up the cat, cradling him in my arms, and walked to the sunny front steps. I sat with him for a few moments. Rubbing his ears, I felt the rises of scarred skin from past fights. Usually he enjoyed his petting, but not today. He kept looking about, into the yard's shadowed corners, searching for something. He too, seemed anxious to be busy, cleaning up, doing domestic chores. Like the rest of the neighborhood, he was eager to get going with the work.

In the past he would not have hesitated. Before his surgery he would have been out there, searching through the alleys and yards for his friends, looking for a new love, hunting, and always spoiling for a tussle with a competing tom. That was before—before he went under the knife.

Four years ago he came home after a two-day absence, the left side of his face swollen. A dried eyeball dangled from its socket. The vet suggested he be neutered while in surgery. Without thought I agreed.

"He'll make a much better pet," I remember him saying.

That phrase, "much better pet," turned out to mean a large black cat that now does, mostly, three things: sleep, eat and hunt. Sex was no longer an option. It was as if he put it out of mind, passed beyond this deep drive that, heretofore, took so much of his energy and time. He gave up a world of sex for a world of work. (What would Freud and Marx say about that?)

Since the surgery he has rarely left the yard. His world has shrunk. Now his adventures concern killing wildlife—songbirds, squirrels, and rabbits mostly—that sometimes, cross our lot lines. He tends these lines, like a soldier on duty.

Are neutered cats all like that? Do they lay waiting for hours hidden in the low boughs of spruce trees, watching for the fledgling wrens to topple from their nests and glide like paper airplanes to the ground? Do they slowly stalk gray squirrels, patiently waiting for them to come down from the trees so they can easily be captured on the lawn?

This is what our cat does. He works hard at it, bringing his prey to the back door at times, as if offering it to us. Usually, though, he eats his fill first. Since the surgery we have had to buy less cat food. Yes, he's a hardworking cat. While my sweating neighbor with his fence-painting chore has white paint specks on his face, my cat has blood on his.

Working pets, people say, are out on the farms. I think of those sheep dogs in Scotland, of how they love to tend the herds. Then there are sled dogs. They seem to live to pull. Are our neighborhood pets like that? Maybe this is why we keep them. Maybe this is why we love them. They're not cheap, not anymore. An entire industry is out there—the large warehouse pet food stores are big business today—and you know how much vets charge. I paid over one hundred and fifty dollars for the repair job on the eye and the neutering. Years ago I never would have agreed to that. We have spent a lot on this black cat.

Maybe they do look like us, behave like us. Cats in our neighborhood live in our houses, even sleep with some of us. They pad about on jute-backed pile. Yet, I still have those awful images of the kill—when this cat is crouched over the still throbbing chest of a robin, how its single eye gives it away. At the time of the kill our *Feline domesticus* turns into a panther feeding in the jungle.

Maybe this is why we keep them. Cats, even neutered ones, live in two worlds. They are tame yet enjoy the pleasures of the wild. They cross over at will. We humans don't do that, do we? Cats can be thoroughly ensconced in civilization one moment, eating the latest, most expensive cat food (packed in hermetically sealed plastic pouches) yet can be called back to the wilderness by a birdsong.

Surely we humans are not like this—on the hunt each day (or night), working, working, working. Maybe some of us look like our pets, but we are of a different species, of a different biology. And our behavior is different, isn't it? Pets were put here for us to use, weren't they? Maybe that kid on the bike looks like and behaves like his dog, but do I look like and behave like my cat? Hey, the cat is neutered.

Oh my, what spring can do to a person's mind! Sometimes we do too much thinking, too much pondering. Who cares if we look like and act like our pets anyway? Maybe it's just that they're all around here in the suburbs. I see pets everywhere. Sometimes the neighborhood seems filled with them. On rainy days and all winter long, when out on my daily walk, I see them peering out of picture windows as they sit passively on davenport backs. They wait for spring, for sunny days. They wait to get back to work.

And yesterday they were out in their yards with their owners. Most people were busy, their pets taking part in different ways. Some folks, however, chose to enjoy the day differently. They sat in resin lawn chairs on the cement driveways in front of their open garage doors, and some brought the chairs to their front lawns. Like their pets, they watched movement on the sidewalks and street. They were enjoying the spring sunshine as they relaxed, lazily stretched, and studied the change of seasons.

Some neighbors held their neutered cats in their laps, together enjoying the day. And yes, in those moments, in those poses, they did look alike, behave alike. All their needs were met. Comrades, they sat there, looking out at the world, some perhaps, oblivious to the passing day, dreamily watching a fluttering wing, an errant passerby.

æ 5 ‰

Woodchucks

Once upon a time I dreamed of becoming
a great man. Later, a good man. Now,
finally, I find it difficult enough, and honor
enough, to be—a man.

—Ed Abbey, 1989

HARDY WEINCRAFT BENT OVER at the waist to view better the row of parsnips. It was only the end of the row that had been molested, the end near the fence where the lilacs grew. The fence was of soft number two pine, nailed onto untreated cedar posts. It had been covered with redwood stain, now faded, and the dark green of the lilac leaves made the red boards appear deeper and richer then they really were.

"Hmm," Hardy pondered, hunkering down to have a closer look. "What now? Rabbits? Since the cat died the rabbits are taking over."

The damage was trivial—a few parsnip plants nibbled off—yet the indifference of the act moved in on him like a stifling summer wind.

Suburban rabbits, of course, see food and proceed to eat it. They care not at all of an aging man's wishes. Hardy's mind flashed to the morning paper in which Andy Rooney complained about how nothing was the same anymore; nothing was as it should be. Andy Rooney was an aging critic of the trivia of life, a columnist always harping, always complaining, and always growing older.

Perhaps it started in spring when Hardy planted the garden, but then who could say when deep, important changes really began, especially the slow but sure changes that moved towards you like quietly lengthening autumn shadows? You see them coming but you don't see them coming. They move towards you with their steadily increasing presence until at last you must admit their arrival.

Hardy rose slowly and tilted his glasses to study the rest of the garden. Fifteen years ago the heavy black plastic framed lenses suited his eyes, but they no longer cleared his vision. Just that morning as his wife, Marcie, was primping at the kitchen mirror before she left for her job at Sears, she chided him about the old-fashioned frames. She did not say anything aloud but her quick glance as he wiped the lenses in preparation for his day was enough. Get some new ones, Dad, her eyes told him. He suspected she was concerned about style and fashion rather than his eyesight. Barry Goldwater and Buddy Holly frames made it in the 1950s but had long become *passé*. Even Andy Rooney would have given up heavy black frames by now.

Marcie mentioned Hardy's growing penchant for going barefoot as well. His more frequent refusals to slip on shoes when leaving the house for brief moments bothered her. For this message she chastised him openly, accusing him of dragging dirt onto the kitchen floor. He couldn't recall when it began, his running out to the mailbox in bare feet, then to the woodpile, and now the garden. He even did it in winter, actually enjoying the tingling and numbness on his soles during these quick trips outside. He supposed his Germanic ancestors often went barefoot. He was perhaps, beginning to understand who he had really been all these years. Besides, this soft garden soil felt good under his tired bare feet.

The garden was a small one. It lay at the back of the lot beside the washline poles and garage. In the past when he moved the family to the suburbs, he gardened with a determined seriousness. Then he planned it all on paper and had his seeds ordered before the end of January. In those years every square foot of the plot was tilled and the plants stood like disciplined soldiers in neat, carefully spaced rows. He would help Marcie can some of the produce and freeze some of it too. He carried sacks of tomatoes and cucumbers to the neighbors, whether they wanted them or not. Like a vegetable monger who strangely gave his produce away, he left green peppers, rhubarb and winter squashes on their doorsteps. In those years he gardened, fed the family, and gave the surplus away.

Now, Hardy thought, the rabbits are taking the surplus. But *what* surplus? The past few years his gardening fire was smoldering. The fire that burned inside him—the desire to study seed catalogs and watch the plants grow—was still there, but it wasn't the same. Its flames were a different color, its heat of a lesser degree. The usual surplus of tomatoes, broccoli, green beans, and peppers had diminished sharply these past few seasons.

Hardy found himself planting more and more flowers, and flowers were too beautiful to cut and give away. And two years ago when his next door neighbor, Arthur Treblecox, sold the house and took his bride (as Arthur referred to his wife) to the new condo complex on County Road B, Hardy changed a bit more. The Treblecoxes had been married for over fifty years, were in their eighties, and were tired. Hardy and Arthur had gardened side by side at the rear of their lots for seventeen years. Their summers were largely spent in the back yard at work, comparing new varieties of tomatoes, lettuce, summer squashes, and more. Therapy? A labor of love? Agrarian instincts?

They both seemed to thrive, like the vegetables, from this farming in the suburbs. But the time came to end it for Arthur and his bride. Now the garden next door stood tall with weeds. The new owners, a young couple from the city, were too busy to garden. Now Hardy had

45

weeds, rabbits and new neighbors who preferred to sit indoors and watch cable TV.

Focusing his eyesight, Hardy surveyed the entire garden from his place by the parsnips. Ragtag. He concluded it was a ragtag garden, of the sort Peter Tumbledown—a cartoon character in a magazine of his youth—would have had. The magazine was *The Country Journal*, and it was not just poor Peter Tumbledown's garden that was weedy and unkempt, his barn was falling down as well, tumbling down. The Peter Tumbledown cartoon strip was used to show how not to do things.

In Hardy's garden there were few rows this year. A tomato plant here, a cluster of cabbages there—a patchwork garden. Was there really no plan? Most gardens, like road maps, led somewhere; told of direction and purpose. Their structure was designed to reach a goal; it had a *movement*. His garden stood still, like the center spot in a stalled storm. It lay, quietly flaunting its directionlessness. A maze way, he thought. An obstacle course. Hardy wondered if the rabbits could even *find* the parsnips two days in succession.

Well, the rabbits would have to go, even though they looked so peaceful as they fed on the clover beside the front pines in misty summer mornings. For years the cat was successful in controlling their population. In fall when Hardy would clean the garage one or two dried rabbit skins were found behind the storm windows along the wall—the flesh eaten away—and in spring the cat would be at the front door with a little bunny, alive. Once, one evening, Marcie opened the door to let the cat in and screamed when it pranced into the house with some sort of small animal in its jaws.

"Hardy!" she yelled, "get in here. What does Doofy have?" Hardy found a small, frightened baby rabbit sitting frozen behind the davenport. He picked it up and after the three youngsters all petted it he released it back into the darkening front yard. In the morning he found the remains of the little fellow in the fern bed behind the house where the cat had enjoyed his catch later that night.

Arthur would have solved the rabbit problem with at .22-caliber pistol, quietly, with only one shot. The rabbit would have died in his glory, sated with fresh greens, and would have been buried right between the rows. But now both the cat and Arthur were gone, Arthur to his condo and Doofy to cat heaven. Last April Doofy was found in another neighbor's swimming pool. Hardy and his ten-year-old son buried him in the garden, the boy knocking together a two-by-four-cross with the cat's name scratched onto it and setting the cross at the head of the grave. This spring Hardy planted a catch of forget-me-nots on the little grave. So, this summer the rabbits moved through the yard at will.

Rabbits and gardens were a traditional combination, albeit a volatile one. Mr. McGregor solved the problem to Peter's dismay. There is little room for wild animals in the city. Hardy thought again of the morning paper that told of a Siberian tiger that had given birth to five cubs at the metropolitan zoo. Last year the same zoo planned to kill one of its tigers by lethal injection because it had no room for the animal and no other zoos wanted it. Finally, after public outcry, a place was found in an animal park in Texas. Hardy wondered about those five newborn cubs, not born to live in the wilds of Asia, but born instead, on the concrete of the local zoo. How incongruous for a Siberian tiger to be born on concrete, he thought, as he dug his bare toes into the loose soil in his parsnips row. He envisioned a time when all tigers would be born and would die on concrete. That's one thing Andy Rooney had not complained of yet.

Hardy brought his gaze back to the garden's center by the short parsnip row and a cluster of broccoli plants. He noticed a large broccoli that looked as if it had been beaten with a whip. Its leaves were broken, battered, some completely missing. This was not the work of a gentle bunny.

Later in the week, on Saturday, as he stood over the kitchen sink, washing the breakfast dishes he spied a brown body flash into the bed of orange lilies beside the garage. Wiping his soapy hands on the dish towel, he gently stole down the back steps, carefully opened the screen door and moved over to the lily bed. That is when he saw the mound of soil beside the garage's foundation that lay hidden by the flowers. Another flash of brown fur and the animal was in the burrow beneath the garage's concrete floor. A woodchuck. So this was his new garden visitor.

Nine years earlier another woodchuck had come to the neighborhood. It dug a burrow under a brush pile behind the garage. That whole area back there, which was full of pine trees, was later developed by a local contractor. A Montgomery Ward's swimming pool, the one that brought an end to the cat, had replaced the brush pile. Three small tract houses replaced the pines. A chainlink fence, a sure sign of progress, thought Hardy in his cynicism, enclosed the entire lot where, years earlier, Hardy's youngsters enjoyed playing amongst the pines.

Hardy and Arthur Treblecox set a steel trap, and in a day or two found a paw with about an inch of a slender arm in it. The animal had gnawed its paw off in order to escape. "Poor thing," Arthur said, "but good riddance. A woodchuck sure can tear up a garden." The rusty small-game trap with its length of chain still hung behind the door in Hardy's garage. He could not recall what became of the amputated paw. Now, standing by the new burrow in the lilies, he wiped the last of the dishwater soap foam from his hands and stepped into the garage to look for the trap.

Just before lunch while drawing a glass of water, he saw the animal thrashing about at the entrance to the new burrow. He hurried outside and unfastened the chain from its nail on the outside of the garage. He held the chain, the trap at its low end, and the arrested woodchuck up in the air to examine it.

Surprisingly, the silent creature intrigued Hardy. Not fully grown, but still as large as a housecat, sunlight reflected off its shiny fur like opal beads from the clear waters of a woodland lake. The animal was clean and neat. Hardy noted that its paws and legs were free from mud, and its face, lips and mouth looked as if they had been freshly washed. Its white teeth contrasted with the rusty steel trap's jaws as the animal slowly bit the steel, protesting the pain in its front leg.

48

Hardy had not been this close to a woodchuck before. The animal's pristine beauty surprised him. No dirty, nasty, brutish beast here, just a quiet animal—it had not let out a single cry from pain nor fear—that wanted to be free to go on its way. "A marmot, this animal," he thought, "really old, going back to prehistoric times." Hardy knew that woodchuck was an Anglicization of an Algonkian word. As he studied this trapped youngster, he saw its large, downward curving snout, so like those drawings of Ice Age mammals in his youngsters' coloring books. "Old, old, old," Hardy said to himself, fascinated. "You are of another time," he uttered aloud.

But, what now? A few years ago it would have been simple. He would have used a shovel to beat the animal to death, then, buried it in the garden. Things were simpler back then, but this time, instead of destruction, he considered how to free the animal. Without a second thought he carried the curled fur ball to the front yard and chained it to a young pine tree. Then after getting a shovel from the garage he pried the trap open and let the freed chuck scamper across the street, into the wooded vacant lot from whence it probably came. Hardy thought that perhaps this was one woodchuck that, after nursing his sore leg, would stay away from this side of the street.

Henry David Thoreau wrote in 1853, about how he came upon a large woodchuck in the wild, sunning itself outside its burrow, and after enough time and patience, Henry had been able to get close enough to the animal to stroke its rich brown coat. Hardy had been tempted to reach out and pet his smaller trapped chuck, but wasn't able to do it. "Do woodchucks bite?" he asked himself.

Two days passed without any sign of the animal. Then, on Tuesday, as he sat in the room overlooking the back yard, he saw something moving in the garden. A large brown woodchuck slowly ambled among the disarray of the black-eyed Susan's, Brussels sprouts, irises, parsnips, green peppers, and tomato plants in the garden nearest the garage. He watched the animal come to a single sunflower plant, about one and a half feet tall, and suddenly sit back on its haunches, freeing its front paws. These were used to turn the plant's already large head, succulent with new small leaves, toward it. In a few moments it nibbled off the several tender leaves at the plant's growing tip. Hardy watched with a joy that might have been interpreted as a resigned complacency.

After eating its fill, the large chuck ambled across the small patch of lawn between the garden and the garage and sat for a moment before the open garage doors where it was joined by a smaller chuck that came out of the garage, then, both walked, leisurely, around the corner of the building toward the woodpile out of Hardy's sight.

Once again the trap was set at the entrance to the freshly dug burrow and that afternoon there was another thrashing in the lilies. This time he popped a bucket over the animal, leaving a hind limb and the trap that held it out while he used a large screwdriver to pry open the steel jaws. He noticed that the trap had broken the animal's leg. Then he slid a lid onto the bucket. With the woodchuck in the covered bucket on the seat beside him he drove the captive three miles out to the county wildlife preserve next to the interstate. After removing the lid, the chuck quickly scampered up the trail leading to an oak grove, the broken leg flapping on the dried ground.

"Go back," Hardy shouted as the woodchuck scurried up the trail. "Go back! There's plenty to eat out here. It's safer here." A broken leg was better than being battered by a shovel.

While driving back home he wondered about what he had just done. He wondered about his ragtag garden, his ragtag life. What was going on? What was happening? Everything was changing. Why had he bothered to save the animal? He would just have to keep setting the trap, for there had to be an entire litter to deal with. And what about next year? Moving one chuck would not solve the problem. Then, in his exhaustion, he wondered if he wasn't tired of it all. He had always worn shoes, planted seeds in rows, been true to his wife, and made the mortgage payments on time. "What the hell," he said, pointing the car back home.

ဢ 6 ෬

Waterbirds

Then he saw that normal was
the rarest thing in the world.

—W. Somerset Maugham, 1915

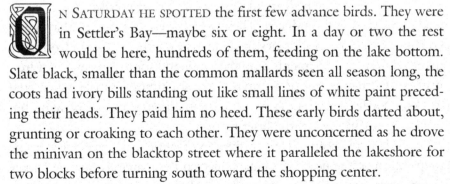

O N SATURDAY HE SPOTTED the first few advance birds. They were in Settler's Bay—maybe six or eight. In a day or two the rest would be here, hundreds of them, feeding on the lake bottom. Slate black, smaller than the common mallards seen all season long, the coots had ivory bills standing out like small lines of white paint preceding their heads. They paid him no heed. These early birds darted about, grunting or croaking to each other. They were unconcerned as he drove the minivan on the blacktop street where it paralleled the lakeshore for two blocks before turning south toward the shopping center.

For the past few years, he had watched their coming and going, even mentioning them to a neighbor now and then. They came in early spring, heading north, and appeared again each fall, heading south. Depending on the weather, they stayed a few weeks, only to disappear as suddenly as they arrived. Few humans seemed to notice, or at least show an interest, for his attempts at conversation went nowhere. Each spring and fall he managed to spend more time with them, sometimes simply sitting for a few minutes, on his way home from work, in the minivan beside the street where he stopped to observe the birds floating on the water.

He did not question his fascination with them. Perhaps it was because he was with *people* all day long, year after year. In his high school teaching position—his administrative superiors liked to remind him—he was expected to prepare students for their jobs and careers. Sometimes he feared the entire American educational system was geared to that goal. The World of Work, it was called, and it demanded well-prepared students. He feared that too many students were developing a workman-like mentality, focusing on such things as punctuality, office dress codes, and profit motives.

But maybe he was just interested in the coots because no one else seemed to notice them. People were busy. They went about their work, driving their vehicles out of the suburb each morning and returning each evening, on time, Monday through Friday. They had little time to stop to ponder these unusual small, black visitors from distant lands.

At the library he learned that coots were also called pond crows, water chickens, and mudhens. They were largely vegetarians that bonded into pairs for mating, nesting and rearing their young. Courtship involved darting movements atop the water and sometimes even a water-walk with attempts at foot stomping. At these times the male issued bold clucks at the female while she watched, sometimes dove out of sight, but eventually acquiesced to the brief mating.

He read about a distinct division of labor that was evident in the preparation of the nest. The male collected the materials but the female constructed the nest. He brought dead vegetation to her, and she anchored it on floating masses of water plants out on the lake or at the shoreline. Sometimes it was built in the open, other times in cattails or bulrushes. When finished she laid eight or ten pepper-spotted, buff-colored eggs. Both parents defended the nest boldly, although losses to shoreline marauders, like raccoons, were common. Incubation took twenty-four days, and both parents busied themselves with raising the young.

Some writers described the parents as wearing a grey, monk-like plumage and who were, at times, gregarious clowns that could become fierce in their defense of the nest and their young. The parents taught the young how to find food, how to dive for underwater plants. The young soon developed the long legs of their parents, with a vertical rudder on the center toe of each foot. The chicks were usually flying by eight weeks, the time when their early brown feathers turn to gray.

He was intrigued when he read that in the western world they were considered a trash bird, hence the derogatory label, pond crows, and that one hundred years ago mudhen shoots would be held throughout the country to reduce their numbers. Prizes were sometimes given on these weekend festive affairs for killing the most birds. Rarely collected and removed, the birds' carcasses were left on the water. The killing was justified, it was said, because coots were taking over the areas of the other more acceptable waterbirds. Coots were felt to be expendable.

They congregated in cold weather in flotillas that could reach the thousands. With the coming of fall, these masses migrated to warmer climes. In late fall, a northern lake could be crowded with them one day and empty the next. Long distance travelers, they were at home in North America's arctic and sub-arctic regions in summer and in California and the Gulf Coast in winter.

He was fascinated with this wealth of information on a bird no one seemed to watch but him. Someone had taken the time to study these birds. No doubt there were wildlife biologists who still studied them, felt they were worth the time. He imagined such a person, someone who spent days and days in the marshes and on the lakes and ponds, alone with the coots.

Today he drove right home and pulled the Mazda minivan into its garage stall and entered the house. His wife would not be home for another hour and a half. He took his school clothes off, stripping down to his underwear, and went down into the basement. He rummaged about for their son's rubber wetsuit, the large one he bought years ago and left there. The boy was now gone, living with his wife and children out West in the mountains of Utah. After pulling the rubber suit on he found the fins, snorkel, and goggles and returned upstairs. Before stepping out to the garage, he slipped on his running shoes. Then he left a note on the kitchen table for his wife that said he was pedaling to the lake and he expected to be home by 5:30 p.m., in time for supper.

In the garage he went to the old balloon-tired bicycle, put the fins, snorkel and goggles into its wire basket and proceeded to pedal the block and a half to the lake.

At first the birds swam away from the slow moving large black body. They seemed circumspect, keeping their distance. So, he floated on his back, treaded water, not wishing to force their acceptance. When using the snorkel he marveled at their black, webbed feet. Deftly, clearly at home in the water, the coot feet were precise in their movements—clear in their purpose. Under the water through his cloudy goggles he saw the feet move away as he slowly approached.

For thirty minutes he floated near the shore of the bay trying to force the issue. Then, thinking it was enough, slowly moved to the shore and slipped out of the water, removed the flippers, tied on his shoes and mounted the bicycle to pedal home.

The following afternoon he was back. Again the coots moved away, but he persisted. Another half hour, another exit, and another short ride home. This is the way it went for a week. Then, finally, he was able to get closer. By Tuesday he felt acceptance. No longer did they immediately move out to deeper water when he entered the lake. They were settling down, beginning to lose their fear. By Friday afternoon he could quietly float within ten feet or so before the birds smoothly paddled away, keeping out of touch.

On weekends he stayed away. These were the times for the citizens to come forth, to use the water. He stayed at home, occupied with yard work, running errands, helping his wife with other things. It was only from Mondays through Fridays that he donned the black, rubber suit and pedaled the bicycle to the water.

The next Tuesday he was able to get closer. Only a few feet away now, the coots went about their business, diving for underwater plants, clucking at each other, and it seemed, at him. When floating on his stomach he peered into the water, observed their undersides, watched their dark legs and webbed feet push the water to direct their movements. And when floating on his back he turned his head to watch them, topside.

Finally, near the end of the third week, he felt even more accepted. The birds did not swim away when he entered the water. They clucked at him, a welcome he imagined, then went about their feeding. He floated out to be with them, to spend an hour on the water in their midst. Now some birds accidentally bumped into him as they moved in search of food, swam over to look at him with cocked heads, their white bills sometimes glistening in the late afternoon sunlight.

He continued the routine for another week even though the water was beginning to be uncomfortably cold. On Thursday, in the first snowfall of the season, he felt a stirring in the birds. Soon they would be gone, he knew, traveling to a more southerly lake downstate or maybe even in Iowa. They would lift off and be gone.

And so it happened. It was Friday afternoon when they left him, but not until they gave him a pleasant surprise. Unannounced, about twenty minutes after his arrival, the birds came together, suspended their feeding and crowded around him. They offered an unusual chorus of clucking, much louder and more persistent than ever before. He felt certain it was directed at him, and he felt inadequate in his ability to respond.

When he had first slipped into the water, weeks before, he was careful not to make any noise, fearing it would drive the birds away. It was only after they started to accept him that he dared to imitate their calls. He tried to cluck as they did, conversationally, but felt his attempts were poor duplicates. So he did not try to call to them often. He settled into a routine of simply watching and listening.

But today, finally, he joined in the chorus, attempting seriously to duplicate their clucks, to make the guttural click they made. And the birds seemed to acknowledge his voice, for after a few of his feeble attempts, they all grew quiet and listened to him. They milled around his large black, rubber-covered body, stretching their necks to peer at his face, to better see this person who spent so much time on his back.

Then, almost suddenly, after he tired of the game, when he stopped clucking, the birds bunched even closer to him, still silent. This time their bodies, even more than before, crowded next to him. He felt there were perhaps, six or seven hundred, all bunched together in Settler's Bay on this gray, overcast late October afternoon.

Then liftoff occurred. He thought it started when a single bird, one at the outer edge of the large black raft on the water, stood up, flapped its small wings and in the coot fashion, ran on the water's surface until it rose into the air. Within seconds all were airborne. When he turned over to better see them, he noticed how they flew in unison out over the center of the lake, then, came back to the bay, made a low circle over him before rising higher and higher as they turned south. He watched their dark mass grow smaller and smaller before it finally was lost over the tree line.

Understanding that they were gone, he slowly swam to the shore where he removed the goggles, pulled the rubber hood off his head, then slipped out of the flippers. He put on his shoes, mounted the old balloon-tired bicycle and pedaled home.

His wife was glad it was over, this swimming with the coots. She did not object to his going to the lake, seemed not to be embarrassed by that, perhaps found it interesting, even intriguing. After some time she could mention it to her friends at work. At first they thought she was kidding, talking quietly about her husband, how after his day at school, he would put on that rubber suit and pedal to the lake. But they respected her, perhaps even identified with her quiet acceptance of her mate's unusual behavior.

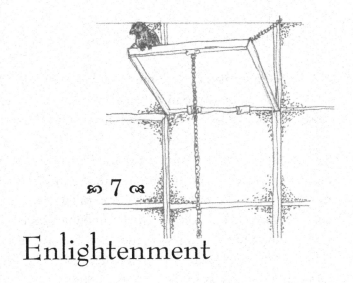

☙ 7 ❧

Enlightenment

Intercourse with human beings
seduces one to self-contemplation.
—Franz Kafka, 1946

IN MINNESOTA, NOVEMBER is like March—both are times of
change. But unlike March, November leads to the cold of winter rather than the warmth of summer. November is also a time
of movement. Field mice scurry about to line their burrows, the black
Arctic coots stop by on their way to more southern climes, and our relatives from the north drive down to The Cities for one last shopping
trip.

Last Friday afternoon upon returning from the office, I sat in my
study reading *Henderson the Rain King*. I watched an early model, oil
burning, blue Chevrolet ease down the street and turn into our drive. It
rode low over the rear wheels. I could see three heads in the back seat—
two adults and a child between them—like riders on a slow moving
Ferris wheel. In the front were three more: two youngsters beside an
adult at the wheel.

Soon a small voice came from the back hall. "Anybody home?"

"Yah, yah, come in," I shouted from the front of the house as I closed my book. My seven year-old nephew found me in the study.

"Hi Uncle—we're here!"

"Hey, Rambo—how ya doin'," I replied, as he came up to my chair and I reached out to put an arm around his shoulders. He was a squat, stump-like youngster with a chin full of wrinkles and a short crew-cut. He wore lenses resembling magnifying glasses. Among many, he was my favorite nephew. As I rose I asked, "Was it a good trip?"

"Oh, okay. We didn't even stop anywhere—like Hardee's," he said hangdoggedly as we walked to the kitchen to meet the rest.

"Hello, Millie," I said to the grandmother, my mother-in-law. "Hi, hi," she quickly replied, reaching to untie the faded paisley scarf knotted at her chin. The youngsters found the television and were exploring the channels. "Well, strangers," I continued, "how was the ride?"

"Fine, fine," my sister in-law, Jean, replied. "Where's Sarah—still workin'?"

"Yah, she'll be home after five. And how are you, Izzy?" I asked the other woman, my wife's brother's estranged wife. "Did you do all the driving?"

"Why, sure. I drove all the way. It wasn't bad. No traffic and no ice. I like drivin'."

I measured out the Folger's as the women removed their coats and threw them into a heap in a nearby living room chair. Soon the coffeemaker was thumping in its quiet, muffled way as the water heated and rose through the tube to splash down onto the fragrant grounds. Rambo was exploring the contents of the Coldspot and found the Pepsi on the bottom shelf.

"I'm thirsty," he announced, peering over his lenses at his mother.

"Ask your uncle," she said.

"Go ahead, young man. The trip must have dried you up," I said.

Jean rose from the table and made her way into the living room. As she passed the TV, she asked in a loud voice, "Anybody in the bathroom—baaathroom?"

While the women chatted, I cut some Colby cheese, found the margarine and summer sausage, and set out a stack of Roman Meal. Soon I was filling cups with the hot coffee. The little kitchen was beginning to smell good.

"Where's the Sunday paper?" Izzy asked, rising from the table with cup in hand.

"Over there by the rocker, on the sewing machine," I replied, pointing the way with my chin.

"No K-Mart ad?" her voice soon called from the other room. "Where's the K-Mart ad?"

"Oh, I must have used that for the garbage," I said.

"Garbage? K-Mart ads for garbage? You should use the Want Ads for that."

"Well, come on, let's go," Jean broke in as she returned from the bathroom, straightening her belt line. "Finish your coffee, Ma. Come on kids—let's go to Target, so we'll be back when Sarah gets home."

Almost as quickly as they appeared, they were gone. Only their battered suitcases, a filled plastic laundry basket, and the partially emptied coffee cups told that they had been in the house. They barely dented the bread, sausage, and cheese.

I returned to my reading chair. As the Chevy backed out the driveway and chugged up the street, my book felt welcome in my hands, so welcome that I opened it and pressed it to my face to breathe deeply of its paper and ink smells. It was special and gratifying, like a cold washcloth on a hot July day. "Henderson, you fool," I muttered as I gazed out the windows. "What are you looking for? You went all the way to Africa!"

November brings darkness. Burrow darkness for those of us who stay. How many Novembers had I seen like this one? How many shopping trips? No men again, I pondered. Where are the men? They come often, these carloads of women and youngsters. They came to shop and to visit.

My wife arrived soon after five, and a bit later the shoppers returned. The rustle of their plastic bags provided a backdrop to the women's greetings. The TV was turned back on, and soon the coffee pot was thumping again. Cigarettes were lighted, and this time there was time for the food.

There is one other attraction in The Cities: Bingo. Big Stakes Bingo. Down here the pots can go over $100,000.00. Each night of the week a special bus circles the suburbs on this side of town and picks up passengers for the forty-five minute ride to the casino south of the metro. The shoppers love their bingo.

After dinner the women were off again—with Sarah—to catch the bus up at the shopping center. I was left with my book, the loud TV, and the three youngsters. Henderson went all the way to Africa, the coward.

Henderson was no competition for the likes of *Sponge Bob*, *Jimmy Neutron*, *CSI*, and the Animal Channel. There was no place in the house that the television did not reach. As I put the book down, my little friend came into the study and suggested it was time to snack.

"Uncle—we're hungry," he said as he peered at me through the magnifying lenses. "Thirsty, too."

It's easy to make popcorn. You heat the oil, pour in the kernels and keep the kettle moving. It's even easier to open Pepsi. On the last trip I stuffed them with popcorn. This time I was told: "No popcorn, Uncle. I'm sick of it." So we settled for pizza. Domino's delivered two of them, with pepperoni and cheese. The coupon kept it under fourteen dollars, not counting the refrigerator's Pepsi.

The ride had tired the youngsters and combined with a few hours of television and pizza, they soon were upstairs in sleeping bags on the floor. I settled for the ten o'clock news in joyful solitude and then turned in.

The following day—Saturday—was K-Mart Day. The women left mid-morning with assurances of their gratitude for my baby-sitting services. "That's okay," I responded. "It's Saturday, and I don't do much on Saturdays." Henderson—did you ever lie?

But this Saturday was to be different. I had spent too many Saturdays carrying out my avuncular responsibilities inside small houses in November, with three and often more active nephews and nieces. My rusty Blazer was soon purring down the street with me at the wheel and my spectacled chum beside me while his two cousins viewed the scenery from the back seat.

"Where we goin', Uncle?"

"Africa."

"Where?" a chorus of three young voices replied.

"We're going to Africa."

"Come on Uncle. Where ya takin' us?" my copilot asked.

"Well all right—it's not Africa, but it's the second best thing, at least around here."

"I know," a voice spoke up from the rear. "The zoo. We're goin' to the zoo!" I was surprised at the youngster's apparent precociousness.

"That's right. Give that man ten silver dollars," I said, consciously referring to an old radio show I knew they had never heard of. "The zoo, the zoo, we're off to see the zoo," I sang.

I don't like zoos. For entertainment, they rate dead last. Too many loud youngsters, too many people—period. Too many pacing tigers, and those chimpanzees that stare directly into my eyes. But this was a cold, overcast November day, and the crowd would be small. Urban dwellers preferred to stay indoors on such days, even if it was Saturday. The zoo was almost deserted, so except for a few stragglers, we had it all to ourselves. An imitation Africa. In desperation I ran off to an imitation Africa.

We saw peacocks with broken tail feathers walking empty-mindedly over gray, hard-packed ground. We saw young gorillas lethargically at play with bright plastic toys, all behind glass. And timber wolves. We found them, but they resembled tame sled dogs as they stared blankly at us, only inches away through the chain-link fence.

61

My nephews seemed not to see what I did. They laughed and shouted as they ran from cage to cage. After the circuit of exhibits, we wandered to the nearby conservatory. "Have you guys ever seen this?" I asked as we began to climb the high, concrete steps. "What is it?" one replied. "A church?"

"A conservatory," I answered. "It's full of fancy trees and flowers. Jungle plants. You ever been here?"

"Nope," my thick-lensed friend said.

"Nope." "Nope," mimicked the two others. "What's it like? I don't like plants and stuff," one declared. "It still looks like a church to me."

We were greeted by a middle-aged woman with her hair done up in a fresh permanent. A pin on her breast said, "Volunteer."

"These guys came all the way from the Northwoods—250 miles—to see the conservatory," I told her, lying again.

"Well, good!" she enthusiastically replied, like a matronly grade-school teacher. "You're just in time. Today is the last day of our chrysan-themum show. Follow me and I'll get you started, then you can go ahead by yourselves." She led us along the narrow, damp concrete walkway through the foliage.

"This is an ancient place," I mused, looking around. Not only ancient, but the building was in an ill state of repair. Paint peeled from the wooden strips between glass panes. It was *old*. One of the South American palms had reached the high ceiling and had been topped. It stood now, headless, a flat stump way up just under the glass. "That's what you get," I said to myself. "You reached for the sun and were cut back. Where were you trying to go, anyway? Stay here with your friends where it's warm. Minnesota is out there, and it's November. That's not the Amazon Basin."

"See that tree?" our guide said, pointing to a big one with roots coming way down to the ground like drooping tentacles. "God made it like that so it could hold itself up in swampy places where the ground isn't solid."

62

With that tidbit of absolutism, she left us on our own. The youngsters soon determined that the pathways led to numerous, inviting green and drippy places and they were gone, out of sight. I struggled for my own solid ground, then momentarily found the boys at the penny pool. "Uncle, you got some pennies? We want to make a wish."

We all tossed coins. Everyone took time to think up a wish and then carefully underhanded their penny. "Why not?" I thought, but all our coins fell on lily pads. None sank to the bottom with the others. "Oh-oh," my little friend concluded. "Now our wishes won't come true." Our pennies lay defeated like staring chimpanzees and tame timber wolves.

Right from the start of our tour I noticed potted chrysanthemums placed along the green exotica all through the wing we were in. How old and domestic the mums seemed! Bright, showy, and without perfume. A tough plant, bred almost to weediness. "Mum's the word," I couldn't resist whispering. Mute mums that look at you in colorful silence. No smell. All show. The flower of our times. A juxtaposition. A flower that lost its essence, yet is propagated and placed on display for the citizenry to enjoy. Timber wolf flowers. "Henderson, did you go to Africa to search for a fragrant chrysanthemum?"

"What a day," I thought. "What a weekend. Shopping sprees, bingo halls, caged animals and now chrysanthemums. What the hell— that's life, isn't it, Henderson?"

Linnaeus would never have approved of this. He knew the worth of the small, fragrant flower. Large showy flowers, finally, although found in nature, were out of place in Minnesota. In this land, they are not part of the natural scheme of things. Leave it to humans to bring us flowers that are big, showy, and without perfume.

The voices of my three charges came to me from the pathway ahead. "Suffer the little children unto me," I thought. I followed their laughter and joyful shouts. *They led me through the maze.*

After another wing of damp, lush tropical exotica, my pathway suddenly opened into a large room full of sunlight. No dense greenery here to reach up to the glass roof and block out the light. It was a warm room, more warm than cool, almost too warm. The light coming through the walls and roof met a new brightness from below, for the wing was filled with chrysanthemums. Filled. They seemed everywhere. A circular pathway surrounded a sunken center area that must have been fifty feet long by thirty feet wide. A sea of color. Reds in all shades, yellows, golds, oranges, lavenders, blues, even chartreuses—a giant psychedelic rainbow laid flat and folded over itself again and again until all its colors were tucked into this conservatory wing. Brilliant luxuriance to the extreme, overdone to the point of ostentation. A silent, colorful wasteland.

Along the outsides of the wing's walkway were tiers and tiers of mums, packed tight. A chrysanthemum climax! The grand finale on the night of the Fourth of July. The brightest of the bright, the loudest of the loud.

Temporarily numbed by this unexpected floral show, I moved along the pathway carefully, to the far end of the wing where, abruptly, a patch of whiteness caught my eye. A large display of mums lay quietly along the east wall. It was a pool of white chrysanthemums: white, puffy flowers as large as new, shiny softballs. Pure white. I stared for what seemed like several moments run together.

My trance was suddenly broken by a gray flutter at the upper edge of the whiteness by the windows. The ancient windows had been cranked open to let in the cool November air, and a sparrow—a bedraggled English house sparrow—had flown into the wing. He perched just above the white flowers and turned his small head to glance down at me. Our eyes met, locked for a moment above the white pool. Here was a grimy, winged urchin, but in that moment, in that instant, he was transformed into something grand. He had flight.

Then, releasing me from his stare, he warmed himself, and flew up like a sudden shaft of white light to another open window behind me, in the west wall. I slowly turned to watch his fluttering exit. It was then that I began to understand. Beside the open window, partially hidden on a wet, drippy ledge sat an aging statue of the Buddha. Made of simple concrete, no more that eighteen or twenty inches high, it sat amongst a small patch of dark foliage where it must have been sitting for years and years. Today it smiled down on me, and the sea of white chrysanthemums.

"The Buddha!" I thought, quietly startled. I met his gaze, then, momentarily turned back to the east and the mums, conscious of the statue's beam of influence behind me.

I was revived by a gentle tug at my hand. "Uncle," my nephew said softly, "aren't these white ones pretty? Mmm—and they smell so good," he continued as he bent to bury his nose up to his glasses in the nearest one.

"Yes," I replied hesitantly, as I stood transfixed. "They *are* nice." And then, with just another little, gentle tug, the boy pulled me down to plunge into the white pool. There was a perfume, a white, bright, enlightening chrysanthemum perfume.

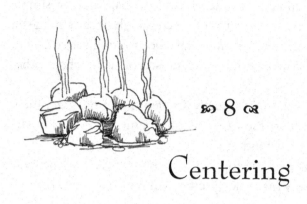

Centering

I had found a strange serenity
in the midst of chaos.

—Michael Van Stappen, 1998

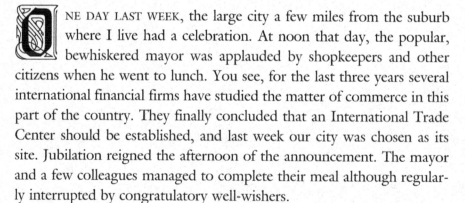NE DAY LAST WEEK, the large city a few miles from the suburb where I live had a celebration. At noon that day, the popular, bewhiskered mayor was applauded by shopkeepers and other citizens when he went to lunch. You see, for the last three years several international financial firms have studied the matter of commerce in this part of the country. They finally concluded that an International Trade Center should be established, and last week our city was chosen as its site. Jubilation reigned the afternoon of the announcement. The mayor and a few colleagues managed to complete their meal although regularly interrupted by congratulatory well-wishers.

It had been a long struggle. Other cities could have been chosen. Ours saw the opportunity several years ago and carefully carried out the early stages of a downtown renewal program that left space for the trade center building in case it were built here. City planners, architects, business people, lawyers, investors, the mayoral staff, the governor's people and many of the educational and professional leaders of the region worked hard. There were headaches, late meetings, doubts, and frustrations.

This was something big. It was part of a developmental process that began a few thousand years ago when a prehistoric tribal community established a village on the same spot. Then came the Dakota, and later, in 1837, a single Frenchman built a log cabin beside the river. Then, on the same site, appeared today's metropolis. The Frenchman too, had good business sense. History tells how he acquired a degree of affluence by operating a still and selling whiskey to the tribesmen that lived along the waterway.

At lunch that Tuesday afternoon last week, prayers were offered over the restaurant tables in thanksgiving for the International Trade Center. In the evening an architectural model of the tall, prominent tubular-shaped building—prepared ahead of time in anxious anticipation—was hurriedly displayed in a plush downtown bank lobby. People came, champagne and hors d'oeuvres were offered, compliments of the business leaders. Onlookers envisioned the completed building. It seemed glorious.

The city is built at the confluence of two rivers. Both are large, major waterways that have enchanted the human mind for hundreds, and possibly even thousands, of years. Some of the region's archeological sites date back to over four thousand years. Sealed entrances to ancient caves, that doubtless were habitation sites, dot the high sandstone banks right in the downtown area, and the tribesmen are still here, despite the enterprising Frenchman. They like to stand, on occasion, on the cliffs to marvel at the rivers, to put tobacco down in honor and respect. In fact, not too distant from the site soon to be filled by the trade center is a small reservation, a tribal nation, carefully located outside the city limits. Only a few hundred people live there, tucked away amongst the rolling scrub hills and swamps that move out from the rivers in that direction.

I occasionally visit the little community since it holds a certain magnetism for me, as it does for several other people, but more importantly because it has a sweat lodge. Most citizens of the United States, I suspect, are not familiar with the institution of the sweat lodge. It's an ancient circum-polar trait found in prehistoric sites in all arctic and sub-arctic regions. It's very old. I suspect Neanderthals used a version of the sweat lodge fifty or sixty thousand years ago, but archeologists have not yet substantiated this.

The little lodge is dug into a small wooded knoll only a few miles from one of the rivers. The land is rolling as it slowly rises from the flat, low valley where the city lies. Scattered oak groves and many huge wild cherry trees cover the reservation. Numerous small marshes and ponds interlace the hills. It is a place where wildlife is still found, although it must compete with railroad right-of-ways, snowmobile trails, high-tension power lines and the usual other debris that rings large cities.

To get to the lodge, one must turn into someone's driveway, then follow the dirt trail to the left, away from the yard, up into the hills as it winds through a dumping ground for diseased elm trees and discarded automobile tires. Suddenly, one finds the little structure, nestled beneath a few large oaks. A small pond nearby is loud with frogs in spring. It is a wooded place, yet still with room to move. The roadway ends near the lodge with a turnaround, and there is room for automobiles to rest just off the pathway in the grass. No towering buildings are in sight. The small lodge looks like a giant, dark overturned mixing bowl, almost hidden in the tall grass under the oaks.

Once a month, several people meet there to sweat. At dusk they strip naked and file, crouching, into the small structure. Several stones, heated to an orange glow in a nearby fire (all under careful ritual guidance) are forked into the lodge one at a time. Then, as the doorway is closed, there is complete darkness, except for the bright glowing rocks in a small pit dug into the center of the lodge floor. There is a hand drum. There is song.

The Manidoog—supernatural forces—are invoked. The spirits at the cardinal points of the universe, plus those at the zenith and nadir, are called as well. They respond favorably and all the community members—past and present—spiritually enter. Finally, all forces of the universe flow into the small, dark, very hot, enclosure, and it becomes the cosmic Center, a place of continuous birth; the primal centerpoint of existence.

The people crowded into this small dark place, squatting in a ring around the hot stones, their dripping bodies pressing against each other, speak in turn about their lives, their loves and fears. They rub themselves with sage. Water is periodically splashed upon the rocks, and once or twice through the sweat the door is opened briefly as an assistant places even more heated stones inside. They are quickly moved with antler tongs to the pit. More water, more drumming, more song. More steam and heat. More sweat, talk, and thanks are given. A pipe is passed as tobacco is offered. The people stay there for an hour, then two. They become one with all.

It is a quest for the center; the spiritual center of existence and it takes place each month in all seasons under the dark sky on the little wooded knoll amongst the piles of elm trees and spent tires. It is done as the people have always done. The ceremony is everything and it leads nowhere. It is all, and it is nothing.

Soon, perhaps early next year, the International Trade Center will start to rise and take its noble place in the nearby city's skyline. A true *axis mundi*, its steel, concrete, glass and plastic tubular form will tower above other downtown structures. Like its small counterpart hidden away only a few miles distant on the wooded knoll, it too, will represent the quest for the *Center*—the inaccessible center of existence. Emissaries will come from all parts of the world, dressed in the proudest finery. They will talk of important things and make far-reaching plans. It will be a hard, tangible, material center, an international trade center, projecting its presence up high and out into the future. *It will be everything*. The people that carry out its rituals will be important people. They will be the movers of the world. They will be the people who are going some-where.

ℬ Country ℬ

℘ 9 ℘

Butternuts

Touch the earth, love the earth, honour
the earth, her plains, her valleys, her hills,
and the seas; rest your spirit in her solitary
places. —Henry Beston, 1928

IN MY MIND THEY STILL STAND, where it seems they always stood, on the rocky hillside in the east pasture on the family farm in north-central Wisconsin, thrusting their roots down into the gravelly earth, their branches reaching up and out into the clean air. There were four of them, clustered together amongst the outcropping of glacial rock. Four members of *Juglans cinerea*, the American White Walnut, or as it was usually called: Butternut. In summer they were nondescript trees with numerous dead branches—dark, dry branches that mingled with the verdure of the living.

In this season, the trees were as much alive as not (if a woodsman trimmed away their dead branches, he'd take about as much as he left). In winter, on the other hand, when they stood confronting the elements without the protection of their leaves, it was impossible to tell the

73

living from the dead, and the trees took on a symmetry again, a wholeness that might have been seen as a pretension that all was well. Ignored by the Holstein and Guernsey cattle that nibbled at the meager grass that tried to cover the rock that was the hill, always passed up by the robins, towhees, orioles and wrens as nesting places in favor of the nearby more protective conifers, they seemed only to exist in their chosen space and to accept their lot: life and death together.

They grew just beyond the northernmost boundary of the climatic zone for their species, and each winter the prolonged frost gnawed at their tissues, but each spring they budded again, trying to recoup what winter had taken. And so they existed, a mixture of life and death, all through my childhood and youth, asking nothing, and being noticed by few.

Their nutmeats, sweet, rich and oily—like hot marrow hidden in the deep tunnels of hollow bones of beef roasts—could be savored only after the expenditure of considerable effort. To taste them, we stained and often scraped and cut our fingers. We—my two brothers and I— would use steel hammers to break their hard, spiny shells. Some years there would be no nuts at all, the trees apparently deciding not to expand any of their precious energy on seeds, that often as not, fell on hard rock and never had a chance of sprouting. But when we found a few of the ripened nuts and struggled to expose their meats, it was like tasting a well-kept secret.

Like the hills, rocks, and the sky itself that enveloped the farm, the butternuts belonged to the outside things, never being taken indoors into the farmhouse. My father rarely talked about them, as if they were among the givens in life, those things that bore little contemplation. Only once did he openly acknowledge their presence. In a late, cool September evening after the milking was over, he and I walked out to the pasture to search for an old Holstein named Zonie, expected to freshen soon, and which had not returned to the barn at milking time. We found her hidden with the wet, steaming calf, amongst the boulders beneath the butternut trees, the placenta in its own warm fog, lying nearby.

"Good," my father said. "We got here just in time. She hasn't eaten the afterbirth."

"Why do they do that, Dad?"

"To clean up the place where the calf was born."

"But why?" I asked again. I was twelve, and while having witnessed many such births, I had never before thought to ask why the cow usually tried to eat that large, slippery, slimy mess—the afterbirth.

"Well, it's really pretty amazing," he said. "Cows are plant eaters, never intentionally eating meat except at the time of birth. It must be an instinct that goes way back to the times before cattle were domesticated, when they lived in the wild with their predators. They always try to hide their newborns to protect them so other animals won't know a birth took place. They get rid of the evidence. They lick up any blood and actually swallow the afterbirth. When you think of it, it's probably something millions of years old—something that goes way back. It's about survival and how things struggle to stay alive."

As he spoke his eyes found the trees we were under and his head tipped back to survey their branches. "Look at these old butternut trees," he continued. "They've been here as long as I can remember, trying to stay alive, and just like old Zonie, they've succeeded. There's something inside things that helps them cling to life."

My mother too, knew that the trees were there. Most days of her married life, more than forty-one years of them, she saw them from the window above the kitchen sink where, off in the far pasture they stood, pulling her eyes to them. But she did not put their message to words. Mother was an inside person, coming to the farm from the city at the age of twenty-one, newly married, and three months pregnant. While she openly showed her love for my father, her disdain for the rural life was always, like the rocks of the hillside, deeply buried and only occasionally visible. She kept the house immaculate, and even though we lived only a few steps from poverty, always found some money from the monthly milk check to replace worn furnishing when needed. To walk into our house, our closest neighbor, Fred Schillingbauer once said, was like walking into the window of Wilbeck's Furniture Store in town where everything was new-looking, and in its proper place.

During those years on the farm, the 1940s and 1950s, my brothers and I were young, and in our innocence thought little of life and its opposite. The butternut trees were just there. As the years wore on, we found less time for them and their sporadic fruits. Grade school gave way to high school with its driver's license examinations to pass and girls to date, basketball and baseball games to win, and in our own private lives, facial hairs to wait and hope for. The outside world occasionally reached into our fields and did some reaping of its own, as when the oldest Schillingbauer boy, Michael, went to Korea and never returned, his memory marked by a six-by-eight-inch brass plate affixed to one of the pews in the Lutheran church in town.

Mother died in 1978; father two years later. The farm passed into strange hands. My brothers and I all managed to struggle through college and in the process, scattered, like seed, each to our own adult hillsides with wives and sons of our own. Rarely do we see each other.

YESTERDAY, ON THE WAY HOME from the urban high school where I have taught for eleven years, I saw an old green pickup and its older occupant parked by the freeway at the edge of the black-top service road. On the hood was propped a cardboard, hand-lettered sign: Butternuts. When I walked from my car back to the truck I found a man wearing a tattered red-and-black-checkered shirt, faded blue bib-overalls, and high-top black work shoes with worn soles curled up at the toes. He sat on the dented, rusty tailgate. His lower face was covered with white stubble of whiskers that told of the coming end of things, but above them gleamed clear blue eyes that sparkled like eternity. He looked at me from rocky hillsides.

Beside him were two wooden peach crates, their newly cut pine boards bright to a near whiteness. They had a rich, pitch-smell, strong and natural. A mountain cougar bared his teeth on the colorful labels on each end shouting: "Colorado Albertas—Cling." Inside, heaped to a high, rounded pile were butternuts, their green-black fuzzy coats still intact.

"Seventy-five cents a pound, or two dollars a box," he said before I could utter a word.

I saw 1952 Chevrolets, young men wearing Milwaukee Braves baseball caps, younger rouge-cheeked girls with white blouses whose sleeves were tied just above the elbows, and metal plates secured onto the ends of church pews. Taking a few nuts into my hand, their sticky shells adhering to my palm as I closed my grip again and again, I was suddenly far, far away. The distal tips, the ends that grew away from the tree, were sharp as needle points, just like they always had been.

Noting my interest, the voice from the past said, "I'll give you both boxes for three-fifty. They're good eating."

Carefully placing the nuts back into their box, I said, "Yes, I'll take them both."

ஐ 10 ଔ

Blue Cows

Listen. Below us. Above us. Inside us.
Come. This is all there is.

—Terry Tempest Williams, 2001

EVERYTHING'S MODERN NOW," he said, more to himself than to me. It was our neighbor, Jess Mughlow. I had watched him through the grocery store window while waiting for Mrs. Burrows to bag my few items. He walked around the family's new 1952 Chevrolet Impala sedan, its fins nicely flared with the look so popular in those years. As I came outside, groceries in the crook of my arm held at my breast, I must have been nearly beaming, expecting to be grilled about the car—How does it ride? Is there room in the back seat? Is it a six or an eight?—but upon seeing me, Jess stood back and uttered a quick "Howdy." Then he slowly said, "So this is it. Looks nice." Pausing another moment, he glanced to the shiny car and said simply, "Everything's modern now." Then he quickly touched the greasy bill of his cap with his right fingertips, turned and walked off to the post office.

I drove the few miles home, a bit miffed. After all, he could see I wanted to talk about the new car, and no harm could come of that. Still, I smiled, for I had always liked Jess. He and his wife were good neighbors. They were unassuming friends. Jess, in particular, was rather plain looking, usually wearing blue bib overalls, a plaid flannel shirt and the blue denim farmer's cap that I thought, when younger, that all men wore. When Jess looked at a person he tipped his head forward, tucked his chin against his chest and peered over his wire rimmed glasses. He was an expert in expressing himself in single words, or at most in a short phrase. Rarely did he use a complete sentence.

Old fashioned? Conservative? Perhaps, but it was not that he refused to accept the new because he occasionally would. Instead, he preferred to live his life and to keep on doing things the way he always had, and the way his father had before him. The Mughlow farm had been in the family for three generations, and while the neighboring places changed with the times, the farm itself seemed almost to stand still, like a stubborn grandparent, refusing to be caught up by the changes that came to the county after World War II.

Steadfast—that's it, I thought, slowly taking the Chevrolet down asphalt-covered County Road D, through the mile-long white cedar swamp between the tiny town and the hilly farmlands to the north. *Jess is steadfast, just like his farm,* I concluded, almost fascinated with the concept.

For this, perhaps, he might have represented some sort of threat to the other farmers. They were working long hours and hard hours, seven days a week, caught up in the desire to improve things, to increase milk production, to better their herd's butterfat content. Jess had excess acreage that could have been cleared for cultivation so his herd could have been enlarged, but he refused to break new ground. He cultivated only the fields his father and grandfather had cleared—no more, no less. He kept about fifteen head of milking cows, while his neighbors tried to keep twice that number in production year around.

Along with his steadfastness, Jess had something else that made him stand out. He owned a herd of blue cows. They really weren't *blue*

blue of course, but that's what my dad called them. The Mughlow herd was a color that would result if you mixed purple, blue, and a light metalic gray. His cows had the markings of Holsteins: a white background with splashes of the darker color, but instead of the bright black of Holsteins, their markings were this unusual blue color.

"Look at those cows," Dad commented one day as we drove past the Mughlow place. "Jess must drive Arnie nuts."

Arnie Mitterand, the County Extension Agent, was a real force for change. Ever since the late forties he had worked to improve the income of the dairy farmers. One thing he pushed was artificial insemination. After the war, artificial insemination became a reality and was instantly recognized as a sensible, inexpensive way to improve herds. In only a few years, a farmer could see the change in milk production. Arnie approved of the new breeding cooperative in Shawano where pure-bred bulls provided semen from several breeds. Guernsey, Brown Swiss, Ayrshire, Jersey, and even some beef varieties were kept, but these strains were not used as much as the popular Holstein, the large blocky, black-and-white breed that thrived so well in the rugged terrain and climate of that part of Wisconsin.

With a telephone call and a small fee, an inseminator would be dispatched to a farm in a day or two. No longer did a farmer have to own his own bull. The cost and danger of keeping such an animal was instantly removed with the co-op. After a year or two, even Jess Mughlow saw the advantages and joined. By the early fifties, pastures had become showcases where cattle could be displayed like sparkling gems for neighbors and other passers-by to admire.

There was something incongruous about the scene. The land was not the best for farming. The soil was light, often sandy, not heavy and rich like further downstate. And there were hills, not tall and menacing, but lower and tightly packed, just steep enough to make a person acutely aware of their grade when maneuvering machinery on them. And the ubiquitous white cedar swamps, often with tiny icy streams that trickled along like rivulets in saturated fields, gave a degree of sedgyness to the farms in lower areas.

This was a northern land, calling for a certain style of life. The new cattle, I thought, were not of this place. They were clean and shiny, like the new Chevrolet—intruders, not unlike the summer people from Milwaukee and Chicago who were starting to appear on the town's main street on warm weekends.

These new herds replaced the smaller multicolored ones of the past. Jess Mughlow was of that past. He was a survivor. He was of the countryside, of the days when life in that part of Wisconsin was slower, more leisurely, and perhaps, a bit more comfortable. All of this comes to me now that I am older and have left the farm.

I recall the summer that Jess bought a calf from us. We experienced a fine spring and had a surplus of young stock. My dad left word at the feed mill that he had some calves for sale and one afternoon Jess's sun-faded and unwashed pickup turned into our drive.

"Bill," he greeted Dad, "understand you have some extra stock."

"You bet. There's a pen full in the barn."

"Mind if I have a look?"

"What do you need?"

"Oh, let's see what ya got."

Jess left with a fine Holstein calf tied in the back of his pickup. Dad felt a bit proud, I think, feeling that he would have a hand in the improvement, finally, of that blue herd. Throughout the summer and into fall we occasionally saw the calf whenever we had reason to be on the Mughlow place. It was growing into a large, strong heifer and would make a solid addition to Jess's herd.

SPRING CAME AND THE MAPLES, clustered amongst the rocky hillsides greeted the warm days with new, soft leaves. Deer came back to the meadows in the evenings when the perennially new earth-smells filled the air. I recall how I would sometimes walk out into the pasture across the road from the farmstead on such evenings and stand, eyes closed, breathing in deep breaths, holding in the air, forcing that primal perfume into my blood stream. I was young, about to finish high school, preparing to leave that life of the land. It was early May, and the snow had left the fields. The drone of tractors could be heard as neighbors tried to get a jump on the spring fieldwork.

One day I climbed down from the yellow school bus and was walking up the long dirt driveway when a car turned off the blacktop. Stepping aside, I waved at Jim Douglas, the new inseminator who served this part of the county. A young man, one who walked faster than the farming people, he had the spark and enthusiasm of the county agent and typified the wave of progress that was sweeping the county in those years, bringing a new vitality to the farms. He might have imagined himself as the missionary bringing the Word to the native village.

Dad was at the barn door and greeted him as he drove up. Jim stepped from the car, shaking his head, saying something about progress. As he lifted the trunk's lid to get his rubber boots and black leather satchel of small glass vials of semen, he said, "I don't know, Bill, sometimes it comes slow. I was just at the Mughlow place. Jess has a beautiful Holstein heifer over there—the best he ever had. Finally, I thought, we're getting somewhere. I was all set to breed her with that new Holstein bull we bought when Jess walked into the barn, looked at me over his glasses and said, "Breed'er Brown Swiss!"

I paused to listen and watch from the house's back steps as Dad and Jim entered the barn, self-righteously laughing as they shook their heads. Suddenly I heard a familiar call above and looked up to see a late flock of Canada geese heading for Canada.

"Everything's modern now," I said aloud, smiling, as I watched them disappear into the blue.

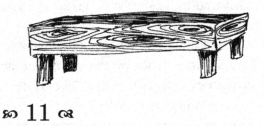

℘ 11 ℘

Polarities

Each of us goes home before his death.
—Loren Eiseley, 1987

ANY, MANY TIMES HE CAME home after his day-shift in town at the crate factory, slowly driving his old sun-baked blue 1937 Chevrolet sedan with the rear license plate five degrees askew, down the farm's long driveway, drunk. How I thought I hated him then, during those World War II and just-after-years. I was in grade school, and he was my maternal grandfather. He was in his late sixties and estranged from my grandmother. She lived with us too, but for the last several years before they both passed, they did not speak to each other and had separate bedrooms.

So, I was sure it was hatred. Yet in all that prepubescent frustration there were times of love. My brothers and I would love him when the three of us gathered around after supper and he told us stories of our father. We barely knew our father—our "real" father as we put it. He died when we were little. Since our new father, our step-father, was away in the war, we lived with my mother and her parents on the old family farmstead in far southern Wisconsin. The fields were rented to a neighbor.

Eino E. Metsa, our grandfather's name, was on the silver mailbox that stood out by the road. Grandpa Eino we called him. "Here comes Grampa, look at him!" we would shout, out of his hearing, when he sometimes staggered from the garage to the house. He had a little room by the furnace in the basement to which he retreated when he had been drinking. If he was really bad, he sat down there talking to himself in Finnish. We would lie on the kitchen floor above, our ears to the register, listening, until our mother or grandmother chased us away. But other times, when we sat with him and listened to his praise of our father, our real father, we would be lovingly quiet.

It was also a matter of fear, I see now, for Grandpa Eino was the only man in the house in those years. He was big, and he was still strong, still able at times to command respect. Each Saturday he brought a sack of groceries home, continuing to do his share to keep the family together. And there were many times when our fear magically dissipated, as when he tried to teach us to count in Finnish. Again, after supper, in the stomach-filled hour after eating, we would sometimes sit in the parlor to listen to the news report from Gabriel Heater. We heard about the battles in World War II. When the radio was turned off, Grandpa Eino would often tell stories. If it was summer, we—my two brothers and I—usually stepped outside to sit in the rusty lawn chairs behind the house under the sappy box elders. He found us and told about long ago, about the times of his youth in the late 1800s, even stories of the Old Country, of Soumi, of Finland.

When at his best, Grandpa Eino was a good storyteller, a spinner of yarns, a teller of tales. He could project us into other times, carry us along with him to dreamy places still alive in his memory. Now I understand this to have been a metaphysics of love. We did love our Grandpa Eino.

"*Yksi, kaksi, kolme, nelja, viisi, kuusi, sietseman, kahdeksan, ykdeksan, kymenta.*" I still hear his voice, counting in Finnish. He never seemed to tire of trying to teach us. Finnish. I think he loved that language. And we learned, as well as our young, distracted minds were willing. We could, finally, count up to twenty, each word pronounced correctly—the first syllable emphasized and the latter ones always falling away. How he enjoyed hearing us say those words!

We learned of the tales of the *Kalevala*, of Vainamoinen, the bearded old-culture hero who chased after the beautiful maiden, Kyllikki,—of his eternal hope for seduction. We learned of Lemminkainen, the young Lappish lad with the far-roving mind, and of Pohjola, that sedgy farm far to the north, and of Soppy Hat and the swan that swam on the black river up there. We were intrigued by the quest to find the *sampo*, that mysterious, magical mill with its lid of many colors, a mill that had three sides—three faces that ground out grain, salt, and money, all in unlimited amounts.

Sometimes we would be on Grandpa Eino's lap—three boys climbing over an old, tired, laughing man. We hugged him and his sharp steel-whiskers scratched our cheeks.

Against our mother's protestations he would take us into the sauna that stood in the unused farmyard beside the pump house. My brothers, being older than I, eventually tired of the hot baths and quit going with us, but I lingered on and would sweat with him. At least once a week—more during the cold times of January and February—he would fire up the sauna stove. Years later, this penchant for the sauna became another behavior that made him even more distant and eccentric to the family.

I recall sitting nude on the pine benches with him (I must have been in the first or second grade), my young cell-dividing body super conscious of the painful, cleansing heat, and his aged cell-collapsing body, seemingly transported into another awareness beside me. He rarely spoke in the sauna. He would sit on the highest bench, leaning forward, forearms on his knees, hands clasped in the prayer-like fashion, head bowed, eyes closed, dripping wet.

At such times I was sure he was praying, so sure that I said the Lord's Prayer to myself. The intense heat, my anticipation, and the two naked bodies—one so young, one so old—took me to the antipodes of my world. It was like I was experiencing heaven and hell at the same time, all at once.

He moved slowly in the sauna, rising two or three times to splash water onto the rocks. And always, near the end, he would take the clump of birch branches hanging by the door and flail his body. The first time I was unprepared. He had not told me that this was part of the bath, or else I had forgotten. His eyes seemed never to open as skin and branches met, over and over again. Not a sound passed his lips during the flagellation. Was he driving something out, or in?

I've come to the conclusion that in the sauna, where body and mind are transcended to another plane, Grandpa Eino was reaching to his inner core of heat, the animal bio-center that is an inferno in each of us, and pulling it up and out to his other center—that timeless, spaceless, awareness of something we call the spiritual side of life. He was joining the two. This union of physical and spiritual was the climax of the bath.

After the birch beating, he sat for a last few moments in silence and then rose to leave. In the sauna's little outer room by the shower stall, after we rinsed, dried, and were covering our nakedness, he came back to me. If only he could always have been the grandfather he was in those precious moments! Serene, understanding, whole. In those few moments he carried me beyond my mixture of love and hate to a beautiful awareness, something I have been unable to locate ever since.

"Ha," he would laugh. "My little *poikka*, was it hot enough for you? The hotter, the better. Now we're ready for another week!"

But the next week, the three young voices would speak again of Drunken Eino as the Chevrolet came down the driveway just before suppertime.

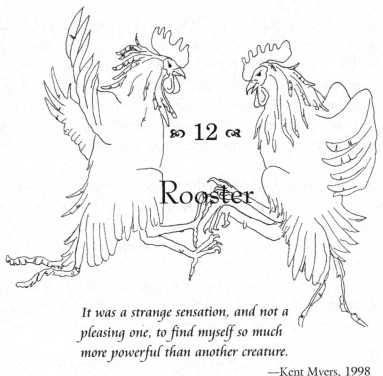

∾ 12 ∾

Rooster

It was a strange sensation, and not a pleasing one, to find myself so much more powerful than another creature.

—Kent Myers, 1998

E'S JUST LIKE A HUMAN BEING, protecting what's his. You can't fault him for that," George Tebbets remarked to his wife, Rachel, at the breakfast table after the couple's two sons left to catch the school bus.

"He's cocky, but I don't want a rooster on the place that isn't," George continued as he poured himself another cup of coffee, his big work-toughened hand completely covering the handle of the small aluminum pot.

Rachel had been reminding him of the trouble their youngest son, John, was having that winter with the rooster. Each day after school, it was the boy's chore to care for the chickens: to feed and water them and to bring in the eggs.

That afternoon the boy, his dark brown hair hidden under a knit cap pulled down over his ears and wearing a heavy winter mackinaw, jeans, and four-buckle rubber boots, carefully stepped over the high sill of the warm, acidic-smelling hen house, leaving the cold January air outside. For an instant he balanced on one foot, using the other to reach behind and pull the door shut. His hands were full, one with a partially filled burlap sack of ground oats, the other with a bucket of icy well water.

At this moment of vulnerability the rooster saw his chance. Being so small, compared to John, he seemed to look for an edge, something to improve his chances in these regular confrontations. Rushing at the boy with one of his mock attacks, as if to jump and perhaps rake him with his spurs, he caused the boy to start, throwing him off balance. With a yell, John hit the floor, smearing an arm and one side of his pants leg with strong-smelling chicken manure. The cold water doused his jeans, the woolen underwear beneath them, and even ran down into his boots.

Quickly rising, he yelled again, this time out of anger instead of fearful surprise, and swung the empty bucket at the escaping chicken. Safely under the roost, the bird strutted back and forth, shouting in chicken-talk while the thirty hens responded in an excited chorus of cackles.

"I'll get you for this, Cocky," John yelled as he quickly opened the door to run to the pump for a second pail of water.

Of all the animals on the farm, except for the bull, John feared the rooster the most. He knew the bull was dangerous, due to his immense size and strength, to say nothing of his unpredictable disposition. But John never handled him—that was his father's job. Furthermore, that huge beast was rarely afforded the opportunity to do anyone any harm. He was kept in the pen in the corner of the barn, fenced in on two sides by thick stone and mortar walls and on the others by heavy steel pipes. He was taken out only on weekly exercise or if he was needed to service a cow, and at such times he was controlled by a rope clipped to the ring in his tender nose.

The situation with the rooster, however, was different. That loud, bold, strutting ego had to be confronted each day, and each day on his own terms. John knew that if it ever came to an all-out battle, the bird would stand no chance. A good-sized stick, garden hoe or other weapon would be enough to dispatch him. But these encounters between bird and boy were never that serious. Rather, they were a matter of pride. No twelve-year-old boy liked to be intimidated by a chicken, even if it was a two-foot-high Rhode Island Red rooster that seemed as fast as lightening, as smart as a fox, and as persistent as a biting black fly.

Hurrying back with the water, John apprehensively kept an eye on the rooster. It stayed safely out of reach, strutting amongst the hens, shouting his defiance, and smartly tossing his head about, causing his pendulous blood-red wattles to flap and jerk like shiny epaulets on the shoulders of an angry, gesticulating Napoleon.

That evening at the supper table, the story was retold for the whole family: the cold water, the soiled coat and pants—all because of Cocky the rooster.

"Roosters are big bluffs," chided Rob, John's older brother. "They don't ever follow through on those attacks. When I used to do the chickens, they never scared me. Remember that Barred Rock we had a few years ago? He was big, but I never backed up from him."

"I'll bet, I'll bet, Big Shot. You don't remember very well."

"Boys, let it be," their mother said.

"Isn't it about time for roast chicken, or maybe some good hot soup?" John suggested. "That rooster would look good on Sunday's dinner table."

"No," John's father laughingly said. "He'll get there but not until spring. We need him. If we kill him now, the eggs won't hatch in spring. They wouldn't be fertile. In spring we'll butcher him. You'll just have to put up with him until then."

As the words settled into John's mind, he calculated that spring was at least three months away. Three months was an eternity to a twelve-year-old boy, especially if it had to be spent being threatened by an overgrown rooster that thought his calling concerned chasing John out of the hen house. If only it was summer! Then the chickens ran loose over the farmyard and took care of themselves. Doing the chickens in summertime amounted to little more than gathering the eggs.

"We could buy some eggs from Mrs. Wisnewski for setting, George," Rachel said. "She has a good flock and always lets a few roosters winter over."

"Yes, we could do that," answered John's father, "but why buy eggs when we can have our own free? Besides, Cocky is a good, big, healthy rooster. His chicks should be the same. No, this spring we'll use our own eggs for hatching. Next year it'll be time to get some new blood in the flock."

John enjoyed hatching time. It was one of the little miracles that regularly occurred on the farm. Last year six hens were placed on straw nests on the floor of the empty corncrib, each with a dozen eggs, and it was John's job to keep them fed and watered. On Saturdays he sometimes sneaked into the crib to watch them sit in their row, quietly possessive.

A strange thing happened to some of the flock's hens each spring: they became cluckers. Some would begin to sit in the nests in the hen house all day, and when approached would make deep clucking sounds. John's mother selected the six finest and put them in the crib with clean, fresh eggs. The rest, after a week or so of having their nests emptied each day, finally gave it up and went back to being regular hens with higher pitched voices.

It took at least twenty-one days for the eggs to hatch. The year before, John missed it all because of school, but forty years ago it happened on a weekend. He remembered the details. It was Saturday morning and while pouring the hens' fresh water he heard the first peep. After running to tell his mother, she came and lifted the hen off the nest and exposed the baby chick, still a bit wet, but starting to dry into a soft, fuzzy yellow ball. Another egg was being cracked by the new life within, and John reached to help break the shell, but Rachel took his arm, saying, "Don't. Let the chick do it."

"Why?" he asked, surprised, looking up to her.

"It's his job. He knows how."

By late Sunday the crib was filled with new life, and in a few days the six mothers could be seen venturing into the farmyard with their new families, exploring the world.

JANUARY PASSED, AND IT belonged to Cocky. He didn't challenge John each day, but his imperturbable presence was always felt when the boy entered the coop. Then, in mid-February something unusual happened. On February fourteenth, John began to befriend the bird. Maybe it was because of the pack of valentines he received that day from friends at school or the good feeling he got when his mother smiled at him at breakfast as he handed her the red heart-shaped box of Whitman's chocolates he secretly bought at the drugstore in town the day before.

Whatever caused the change in his approach to the bird, that afternoon when emptying the water bucket and filling the feeders, John squatted down by the fountain on the floor in the middle of the coop, extended an arm and quietly called to the rooster. Cocky kept his distance. That fall he had been chased through the farmyard too often by John to suddenly be friends with him now, Valentine's Day or not.

But John persisted, each day spending several minutes before gathering the eggs and leaving the coop—squatting, hand extended, trying to tame the bird. By early March, when the sun began to stay a bit longer each day, warming the land and melting the snow on the rock outcroppings on the wooded hills and cattle pastures that circled the farm's fields, the bird began to show signs of settling down and accepting the strange, but quietly gentle, behavior of the boy.

Cocky began to take on a new appearance to John. He really was a beautiful rooster, now fully grown, with the deep, rich brownish-red color of the Rhode Island Reds. His head was massive, its large, clean yellow beak preceding the bright, alert, dark eyes that were surrounded by the fleshy red skin of the face. His huge comb, thick and deep red, fell over to the left. The long, slender and soft feathers of his tail proudly arched in the air. Royalty. That's the image that began to form in John's mind. The rooster was a little king, ruling the flock.

By mid-March he came within a few feet of John's hand, making quiet rooster sounds, while the hens milled around cackling conversationally. But he would come no further, not touching the hand, nor, when John slowly edged toward him, letting himself be touched. It was as if he knew that he was a chicken, albeit a large one and, like the huge Holstein bull in the barn, was part of that other world, not meant to merge with that of humans. He belonged to a place outside of humans.

John wondered if Cocky knew what really happened on the old box elder stump behind the hen house, and if knowing, could ever trust humans. He saw several hens die last fall when Rachel sold a few dressed birds to townspeople. The rooster, who came running at the first loud squawking pleas of the hen's stood at a safe distance, protesting what was beyond his ability to stop.

John recalled the scene. He himself was allowed to swing the ax on a few of the hens. A bucket of boiling water was at the ready. Then after several hens had been driven into the coop and the doors closed, a long wire gaff was used to snag a leg. Loudly complaining, the hen was taken to the stump, her feet and wing tips held together in one hand while Rachel placed the hen's head onto the block. A small twig was sometimes laid atop the head to keep it perfectly still as the ax, lifted by the other hand, came crashing down, through feathers, skin, flesh and bone, biting solidly into the stump. Flipping the headless hen onto the ground, Rachel quickly stepped back not to be sprayed with the stream of blood wildly squirting from the neck as the chicken madly thrashed about before lying on its side, its wings and feet giving the last jerky protests of the killing.

As soon as the ax had fallen—as quick as the hand of a thief in a jewelry store—the family dog snatched the bloody head off the stump.

He smartly stepped several yards away to lay down with the prize between his front paws while savoring the warm, sweet delicacy, and in the process, smearing his muzzle with blood.

The hen was dipped into the hot water to loosen the feathers and soon it was plucked naked by Rachel's quick fingers. With a newspaper torch she singed the sparse thin strands of silky hair off the body before taking it into the kitchen for dressing.

This happened six times in quick succession that day last fall, and Cocky witnessed it all. "Did he conclude about his own inevitable destiny?" John wondered, squatting in the coop, his arm extended toward the interested but wary rooster.

THE LENGTHENING DAYS PASSED as March became April. Near the end of the month when the rain helped bring out the new grass on the hillsides and the warm nights become times for nature to wake up and go about its business after the dark winter, one night the family was abruptly awakened.

"What's that fool dog barking at?" Rachel said, reaching to turn on the bedside lamp. "My gosh, its only two-thirty. You better go see. George—are you awake?"

"Ya, ya," he said sleepily, lifting the blankets and swinging his legs out. "I'm going, I'm going."

He went to the back hall, slipped his bare feet into the waiting barn boots and put his jacket on over his pajamas. Taking a flashlight from the shelf by the chimney that stood beside the back door, he switched on the yard light and stepped outside. The dog, that had been noisily circling the chicken coop in the darkness, ran to the house to lead him to the coop's door.

"What's up boy? What's the matter?" George asked above the din of the cackling hens inside as he unlatched the door. He wasn't ready for what met him. The upper rungs of the roost were lined with hens, but there were feathers scattered over the floor. A hen lay dead under the roost, its bloody throat telling the story. George backed to the door, searching for the mink or weasel with the beam of the flashlight. He intended to return to the house to get the rifle and shoot the intruder, but then the light found a second chicken on the floor. It was Cocky, lying as if dead. Beside him was the body of a weasel with a puncture wound in its face—actually where an eye should have been. The small brown animal was covered with blood. After a few moments to surmise what had happened he used his foot to push the animal out the doorway into the yard. The dog muzzled it but then drew away. Turning his beam back into the hen house, George saw that the hens were beginning to settle down.

Then, standing over the rooster he uttered to the dog, "Well, looks like John will get his wish. This old fellow took quite a beating. If he's not dead now, he will be by morning." He knelt down and saw a gash on one side of the rooster's face that had torn the eyeball out, but it was the bloody wound on the bird's neck that looked the most serious. "Cocky," he said to the still bird, "you put up quite a fight."

At FIVE-THIRTY WHEN THE SOFT LIGHT of the eastern horizon began to push through the house's windows, George and the boys were up, pulling on their boots in the hall, preparing to go to the barn to do the milking.

"Was he beat up bad?" John asked.

"He must have lost a lot of blood. It looked like he was dying, son. I still can't believe a rooster could kill a weasel. That's practically impossible. I've never heard of it happening. That peck to the face must have penetrated the weasel's brain."

Once in the yard John ran to the hen house and stepped inside. After a moment he yelled, "Dad, Rob, come here!"

They hurried to the coop and found him pointing to the top rung of the roost. There, head and shoulders above the waking hens stood Cocky, his body smeared with dried blood, one eye gone but the other open and bright.

"Waahh!" George exclaimed. "Look at him up there—king of the roost! Battered and bloody, but still on top!"

"He's tough, Dad," John said, pride coming through his young voice.

SPRING CAME, AND COCKY, one-eyed and missing several neck feathers, greeted it each morning with his lusty crowing. The chicks hatched in early May, right on schedule. But another little miracle happened. No one mentioned the fact that now the rooster could be butchered. Instead, when Rachel wanted a chicken for Sunday dinner, or when someone from town stopped by for a roasting bird, it was always a hen that went to the box elder stump.

৯০ 13 ০৪

Royal Blue

*One should not stop action until one is prepared
to face an upwelling of thoughts which the act
of living has kept down.*

—Rodney Nelson, 1987

PHIL KLINGSREITER FELT A BIT on edge without quite knowing why. As the fall quarter was coming to an end, his mild agitation began to increase. He went to his classes, tried to be attentive, but the uneasiness persisted. Then, as he pulled away from the parking lot behind the dorm for a weekend visit home, he tried to pin it down, but could not.

When reaching the outskirts of the city the hint of color in the trees caught his eye. It was early October, and he thought of home. The grape vines on the arbors beside the machine shed, where they enjoyed the full summer sun, would look like three blue walls, loaded with fruit. Ursula, his mother, would be sampling it each day to determine the peak time for picking. Every fall she spent several days of hard work—a labor of love she called it—harvesting the grapes, starting a few crocks of pulp for wine, putting up dozens of jars of thick jam and, her specialty, grape jelly.

After an hour and a half of driving, Phil began to let go of the tension of life at the university. He turned onto the macadam county road that led through the countryside he loved. Small diary farms, spaced every mile or so, broke the line of hardwood forest that blanketed this portion of northeastern Wisconsin. He was familiar with every dirt road that intersected the blacktop, with several of the the hand-painted names on the mailboxes that marked each driveway. Here, maples and oaks were more colorful than downstate, further along with the change. Here, the nights already were becoming heavy with dew.

After another half hour of driving, Phil began to relax even more and let himself feel the land he called home. Finally he was turning the 1964 Ford off the road by the farm's mailbox, with the name, THOMAS KLINGSREITER, on it. Here was the beginning of the long maple-shaded driveway leading to the farmyard. And there she was, coming from the grape vines, a small bowl of fruit in her hands held next to her apron-covered waistline.

It was the quiet time just before the evening meal, that time when the cows were in their stanchions, licking up the last of the grain concentrate his dad fed them prior to milking, a few moments before he came to the house for supper. As Phil reached to turn the car's ignition off, he looked to admire his mother with her grapes, her auburn hair in the long, single braid she liked to wear. In that moment Phil knew again she was still beautiful.

"Hello, stranger," she greeted him, walking to the car as he stepped out. "You're just in time for supper."

"Hi, Mom," he responded as they quickly embraced.

"How was it to get back?"

"Oh, all right, but I'm eager to get it over with. I hope this last year goes fast."

Then, glancing to the barn's open door, he asked, "Where's Dad?"

"Cleaning up. Come on. Let's eat." As they walked across the yard's lawn to the house, Phil wrapped an arm around her waist, and she turned her face up to him and said, "The grapes are ready—try some," as she offered the bowl.

"Umm," he approved, tasting one. "The first of the season is always the sweetest." Then he asked quickly, "What's for supper?"

Climbing the few wooden back steps, she replied, "Your favorite—roast beef."

"Well, how's the student?" a voice asked as they entered the farmhouse. It was Tom, coming from the bathroom in his t-shirt, his nose shining, hair wet-combed, and the dark weathered skin of his forearms, face, and neck sharply contrasting with un-tanned upper arms and shoulders.

"Hi, Dad," Phil quickly replied as they shared a brief man's embrace. "I still know when it's time to eat," he offered.

"Come on, come on," Ursula ordered. "Clean up. Supper's ready."

In moments they were at the old round kitchen table, enjoying the evening meal. This was the time to recount the important events of the day, and tonight to hear about school, about how things were going these first few weeks of the fall term. Each had something to say, and all had questions. Then, too quickly Phil thought, he and Tom were out in the dairy barn with the twenty-seven head of Holstein and Guernsey cattle, while Ursula cleaned the kitchen and set some bread. She liked to bake in the evening, saying the night air helped the yeast to do its magic.

The next morning, as usual, Tom rose at 5:30 to do the milking, and Ursula got up at seven to prepare breakfast. Upon completing the chores and turning the herd out to pasture, Tom came to the house, and soon the two of them were at the table, their yolk-yellowed plates pushed aside, their coffee cups emitting wisps of steam. Dust motes danced in the shafts of morning sunlight that fell across the room.

"I should finish plowing the cornfield today," he said, his eyes directed out the window to the field across the roadway.

"Good. I'll start the grapes before the birds get them. Maybe Phil will give me a hand, unless you need him for something," she asked searching her husband's face for a response.

Tom slowly turned his eyes to his wife, as he said quietly, "Urse, why don't you go a little easier on them this year? Look how much is still downstairs. There's just the two of us now, and Lord knows we don't need much. And all that wine. How many gallons do we have? Some of it goes back fifteen years!"

Ursula did not reply, choosing instead to turn away from him to set her sight on the view through the windows. Each fall it was the same. At first the subtle suggestions that maybe there was enough left from last year. Subtlety gave way to persuasion, then sometimes open pleading. But each season, Ursula, like this morning, sat quietly and let them have their say. The grapevines were hers; she had rescued them from years of neglect when the family moved onto the farm back in 1957. She pruned, mulched, fertilized, sprayed and even covered them for several winters until at last they responded to her care and began to repay her with their fruit. She gave them a place, a purpose. They were hers.

Locked in this reverie and struck by the beauty of the yellow birch and soft-maple woods that stood way down along the far end of the cornfield, she quietly smiled and said, "But what would Reverend Schweitzer do without the wine? He says it is the best communion wine he's ever used." As she spoke, she held the end of her thick braid, her gently tapered fingertips stroking its auburn brush.

Tom returned her smile. He thought of Schweitzer—that old perpetrator of ancient myths. Reverend Schweitzer would never discourage Ursula from doing all that work because it wasn't just communion wine that was provided, it was drink for church dinners, items for the fall bazaar, gifts during visitations to shut-ins, and much more. Some of her flowers stood on the altar most Sundays from early spring through late fall, and each year she volunteered a large balsam from the farm's woodlot for the church's Christmas tree. She was, Tom some-times thought, like an assistant pastor in that church. No, if anything, Schweitzer would give his blessings to Ursula's love affair with the grapes. It was as if she had a divine right to do all that work, to turn the basement fruit cellar a royal blue each fall.

Tom smiled again and felt a flow of love going out to his wife sit-ting in the morning sunlight by the windows. He did not know why, but he loved that braid. When he was in the fields and she in the garden it some-times glistened like a star that lingered on into the daylight sky, calling him back to the warmth of the night. In winter, its warmth remained, as it pro-truded from her knit cap, hanging down her back, sometimes nestling melt-ing snowflakes in its crevices. Reaching for the coffee pot, he decided he would let her be, let her do all the canning she wanted. This year he would be a quiet bystander, watching his wife do something she deeply loved.

Ursula called the grapes Concords, but right from the start, Tom suspected something else. They were too small, and their color was not the right shade of blue. He thought they were the lowly Beta, a cross between the Concord and the wild Vitis grape. While having the vigor of a hybrid and the ability to produce a crop under almost any condi-tions, the purists considered the Beta a pauper's grape, only second best, the bastard son of royalty.

A few years ago, the county agent was out to the farm to do some soil testing and before the young man left, Tom asked him about the grapes. The agent took a cutting along and sent it to the university. The verdict: they definitely were Betas. When the letter came and Ursula opened it, she read it, handed it to Tom and said nothing. The subject moved into the past, never put to voice again.

"Hey, it's getting late," Tom said with a sudden jerk, pushing away from the table and rising. "It's time to move the earth."

"Okay," Ursula responded. "Lunch will be ready at noon. Don't be late."

He went to the back hall, put on his jacket and cap and left the house. Soon the faded-red Farmall-M tractor rumbled out of the yard, pulling the two-bottomed plow, its steel wheels complaining as they crunched and squeaked along on the driveway's gravel.

Ursula watched Tom pull the plow across the blacktop road and maneuver it through the narrow gate to the cornfield. Then she rose, went to the upstairs doorway and shouted, "Let's go up there. Your breakfast is cold."

She never did adjust to Phil's sleeping late on his visits home. It was something he acquired during his three years at the university. She knew that wasn't all he had learned, for he stopped going to church as well. Last summer, when she confronted him about this, he responded with a chuckle, saying, "Why should I go to church when there's a basement full of communion wine right here?" She knew there was more than that. Numerous times those first two years, she had scanned a few of his textbooks on weekend evenings. Phil's majoring in anthropology thrilled her at first, until she began to read the chapters on evolution. That's when she put the books down.

WITHIN SEVERAL MINUTES, she had the dining table and kitchen counter cleared and ready for the grapes. She went to the basement, brought up a few dozen small glass jars, the box of sealing wax and the blue cloth caps with their elastic bands—she had sewn them herself— that she used to cover the sealed jars. She quickly washed everything and set the jars on the counter drip board, then placed the wax in a heavy kettle to melt on the stove.

It was close to ten o'clock when Phil rose and came down. Ursula was seated at a mound of grapes resting on newspaper spread over the table. A large yellow earthen bowl sat in her lap as she carefully removed each grape from its stem. Her fingertips were stained a deep blue. On the electric range steamed two aluminum kettles of pulp, and on the counter, hanging from a long-handled brown wooden spoon that was placed between two cabinet door handles, was the first muslin sack of cooked grapes, dripping juice into another dark yellow bowl. The jelly jars sat, lined up and sparkling, like newly polished gemstones, in a tray on the counter, cleaned and waiting for their bath of sterilizing water, and the kettle of melted paraffin rested on a back burner turned on low, waiting to be poured. A hint of cinnamon tried to permeate the humid kitchen air, but its perfume gave way to the pervading aroma of ripe grapes.

"Smell them?" she asked, her eyes sparkling. "There's no smell like that of the Concord grape. Just look at the size of this bunch," she exclaimed, holding up a particularly large cluster. "They're big, but they seem a little smaller than last year. I'll bet it was the dry spell in July. Next year I'll watch more closely. They need a lot of water."

At first Phil did not respond, instead, standing in the doorway, watching a scene he recalled witnessing all through his youth, but not really understanding, he felt, until now. Suddenly the edge he felt yesterday when leaving campus returned. "Ma . . . ," he started to say.

Ursula, not hearing, continued. "Tomorrow I'll get some started for wine, the crocks are cleaned and ready, but today it's jelly. After I finish these two baskets I'm going to get some of those bigger clusters for pies. I'll make them tonight after supper. Concord grape pie, topped with fresh whipped cream—we'll have them after church for dinner tomorrow. King's food, your Grandma Heidreich used to call them."

Phil, looking at his mother, this granddaughter of German immigrants, could not speak. Instead, he thought of a point made the previous week in an anthropology lecture. The subject was myths, their social functions, and why humans keep them alive. "Myths help form the basis for much of our behavior," the professor had said. "To persist, to be useful at all, they must work, not to help the ancients, but we moderns. We need them to move forward, to continue the struggle."

"Will you please get the big old black recipe book down from the cupboard?" Ursula asked, pointing to its location with her chin. "And find the recipe for the jelly."

"The Duchess's recipe?" Phil responded, opening the cupboard door and reaching for the worn, black, ring binder. He came to the table, sat down opposite his mother, the miniature blue mountain rising between them.

The pages were lined school paper, yellowed through time. Recipes clipped from newspapers, written on backs of postcards, and numerous other media, were pasted onto the yellow sheets. Margins were stained with oil, chocolate, and other kitchen condiments that left their colored signatures.

"Where'd you get this book anyway, Ma?"

"My mother. Most of the handwriting is hers. Some of those clippings go back to the 1890s. Be careful. They're brittle. Give it here," she said, extending a hand. "Here it is, Grape Jelly. Look at this fancy penmanship!

> 3½ lbs. Concord grapes (washed and stemmed—
>   include some green ones)
> ½ cup well water
> ½ cup cider vinegar
> 1 tbs. whole cloves
> 1 inch stick cinnamon
> 1 cup raisins

There's a date here—1891." She paused then, still looking at the page said, "Your Grandma must have written this. She got that recipe from her mother, your great-grandmother Heidreich."

"Did I know her?" Phil asked.

"Grandma Heidreich?" Ursula said, wiping a stray strand of hair from her forehead with the back of a hand.

"Ya," he responded.

"No. She died soon after my mother was born."

"Was she the Duchess you used to talk about?"

"Yes, she's the one who left her family's estate in Mechlenburgh to come to America after she married Grandpa Heidreich. He was a gardener there. They eloped."

"How can you be sure of that?" Phil asked, looking at his mother.

"Well," Ursula said, as she looked up at him, her mouth making a surprised image. "We've always known that. She gave up a lot for her man."

Phil remembered how all of this had been discussed over the years. Great-grandma Heidreich, in the process, became known as the Duchess, and this faded and stained recipe for grape jelly was all she bequeathed her descendants.

"Do you really believe this, Ma?" Phil asked, taking his eyes from the worn book and bringing them up to the level of hers. "As if a Duchess would be concerned with making her own jellies."

"Now wait a minute," Ursula answered, still stemming grapes. "In some ways royalty is no different from the commoners. They eat, sleep, walk and talk just like everyone else. Of course a Duchess could make her own jelly, at least oversee its making. Don't let your college education cloud your reason, Phil."

Suddenly it was too much for him. "Ma, don't you see? We don't have to pretend anymore. We know who we are, and it's okay, it's all right."

Ursula was apprehensive about what was coming as she stared reprovingly at her son.

"It's all a myth, a story kept alive to keep us going," Phil said, "to keep us working every day of our lives. Lots of families have a myth like this. It's a great pretension that becomes a veil to hide what our ancestors really were—poor, laboring peasants. She was no Duchess—she was probably a domestic, a maid, if that—and more likely there was no estate at all, just a few acres with a stone building whose ground floor was for the cows and chickens. Maybe she was even illegitimately pregnant when she came to America. She probably ran away."

Ursula's mouth fell. Never before had Phil confronted her this way. A heavy constriction formed in her stomach as she struggled to respond. "Phillip! What's gotten into you?"

"Look at us, Ma. Our relatives have always worked with their hands, not their heads. I'm the first one who ever went beyond high school.

There's no royalty here. We're the people who pay the taxes, not collect them. We're the one's who do the dirty work for society, even going to war when needed, so we can spill our brains, like Uncle Andy, for myths."

"Your Uncle Andy was a good man, don't ever talk that way about him. If only you would work as hard as he did. And there'll never be a smarter man than your Grandpa Heidreich was. Yes, he worked with his hands—you should be proud of that!" She set the bowl onto the table, quickly rose and, wiping her hands on her apron, moved to the stove to stir the cooking pulp.

"Sure they were good people, Ma, but they were also poor. I can still see Grandpa at the supper table that time Grandma made *schwartz-sauer*. Soup made from the blood, head, and feet of a goose. I can still remember plain as day when he pulled that foot from his bowl of black ooze and ate the webbing from between the toes—I'll never forget it! Peasants eating offal like slaves eating rats to stay alive. Who ate the rest of the goose—the white-folks in the Big House?"

"Phillip Andrew Klingsreiter!" she shouted, turning to him, her eyes and mouth wide open, then turning quickly back to the cooking kettles.

"Ma, don't you see how society works? Look at me—how long did it take to get over my illegitimacy? How many years did you try to hide it? Because of some silly social values! I still remember when you and Dad were married, how you took me aside and said that now we were changing our last name from Heidreich to Klingsreiter. You said that from that day on we would be just as good as everyone else, as if we weren't before."

With that Ursula quickly turned from the stove, her braid swinging out in an arc beside her. She rushed from the house, letting the screen door slam. Running to the well in the center of the yard where the lilacs bloomed so profusely each spring, with shaking hand she took the mauve-colored porcelain tin cup they had found hanging on the pump that first day on the farm back in 1957. After checking for spiders, she gave the pump handle a few quick, strong, short strokes.

Her eyes wet, she watched the cup quickly fill from the stream of cool, gushing water. Normally this was one of her greatest pleasures: to stand at the well next to the lilac bushes and drink from the old blue cup—to drink the fresh mineral-sweet water while surveying the farmyard, its buildings, and the surrounding fields, all under a clear sky.

Lightly sobbing, today she struggled to push away Phil's words and take part in this old ritual at the well. After settling down somewhat, she drew a second cup of water and wiped her eyes with the grape-stained apron. It was then that she noticed two Monarch butterflies hovering over the Queen Ann's Lace (Phil always called it wild carrots) growing in the narrow strip beside the chicken coop, where the lawn mower could not reach. The delicate white, lacy flowers opened each spring, and every time, Ursula was sure, the Monarchs found them. But now it was autumn, and the butterflies inspecting the mature seeds would soon start their long migration to Mexico.

As her now steady hand hung the cup back on the pump, she became aware of the tractor's muffled drone in the field across the road. Steadily it went on, never stopping as it prepared the earth's soil for the long winter just over the horizon, and in spring, for the seed Tom would place there in the newly made rows. After the warm rains, that seed would swell into next year's crop.

In frustration, Ursula had not noticed Phil come from the house. Not until he laid a hand on her arm did she realize his presence. She turned to him and accepted his open arms to engage in a long embrace.

"Ma, I'm sorry."

"I lost control," she quietly said.

"No, no, I'm really sorry. I should have known better. I had no right. You and Dad, this farm—all of this is what means the most to me. I'm sorry. I'm nothing without you two, without family, without all this."

"Please, Phil, it's over. Let it be."

For several moments, they stood side by side, each with an arm around the waist of the other with their eyes on the field, the tractor, and the man plowing.

Finally, straightening her braid with a little toss of her head, and dabbing an eye one last time, she said, "I better go in and clear that table. Your father will be coming for lunch."

"Okay, Mom." Then calling to her, Phil asked, "Is it all right if I start picking the rest of the grapes?"

THE NEXT MORNING, Phil rose with Tom at sunrise. Upon leaving the house, they noticed the muslin cloth hanging from the clothesline beside the path leading to the barn. It was stained a deep blue, and in the dawn breeze sweeping the yard, Tom thought it could have been a banner waving from a staff on the wall of an ancient Germanic castle.

"Jelly time," he said approvingly as much to himself as to Phil. "It's grape jelly time."

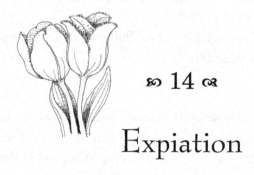

≈ 14 ≈

Expiation

To seek the core of sameness,
the shared identity.

—Edward Lueders, 1982

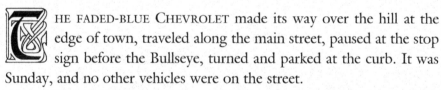HE FADED-BLUE CHEVROLET made its way over the hill at the edge of town, traveled along the main street, paused at the stop sign before the Bullseye, turned and parked at the curb. It was Sunday, and no other vehicles were on the street.

Pierre Clairebeaux Montreal, The Black Frenchman—as some townspeople called him—stepped from the sedan. He retrieved a large bouquet of red gladiolas from the back seat, placed them in the crook of his left arm, then with his right, reached for the large brass key ring at his hip, and let himself in through the tavern's side door.

He was as regular as the mill whistle. Each Sunday morning he swamped out the Bullseye. At the end of an hour and a half or so, he was a bit sweaty, moist under the arms and across his shoulders, and he enjoyed a welcome feeling, a cleansing—an expiation. Working hard, he started a little before ten o'clock, usually when the church bell called the

108

town's worshippers, and finished when the bell rang again as they filed from the church just before noon.

The church, on the rise at the town's west side, was visible from the tavern. It stood, like a sentinel on guard on the hill, its white wooden spire pointing upward, capped by a dark metal cross. Built in the late 1800s of hard, red brick, the building was a landmark for miles around.

The tavern sat in the center of town where the main street ran in what was a little valley. The town was clustered on its gently sloping hillsides, and a railroad track laid down through the town's length, like a long ladder stretched from east to west.

Pierre was the sander at the mill, his bread-and-butter job, as he called it. He stood before his machine, in its drone and dust, sliding the rough plywood panels in and taking them out smooth and fine to the touch. Monday through Friday he was in the machine's grasp. At day's end, a soft pallor of wood dust layered his entire body from cloth cap and uncovered hair to his high-topped, black workman's shoes. The pungent smell of fresh Canadian fir clung to him. The circle of clean skin over his nose and mouth where the air filter's mask was held was the only surface left uncoated, but in the morning he drove into town freshly bathed, shaved and ready for the new day.

He was pleasant to look at. Of medium height, with straight, black hair and clean facial features, he was felt, by most, to be handsome. He spent little time in town except for the eight-to-five job at the mill and the Sunday mornings at the Bullseye. He was not known to mix with others, to find joy in their small talk. His wife, Sarah, herself dark and attractive, used to call him her Louis Jordan, the movie star from France, but that was several years ago. Now in his late forties, Pierre had developed a pre-mature stoop—usually indistinguishable—that hinted of years of work. At times it gave the image of a man who bent to the task at hand. It gave an air of determination to him that, if matched with a brown sackcloth robe, might have made him appear as a monk who each day stole into town, went about his duties, and in the evening retreated to the small farm in the country.

It was becoming difficult for most townspeople to remember the times before the Black Frenchman. Some said an aged Welshman, bent like a winter cornstalk, was the swamper then, but few were certain.

Pierre had a serene air. Sarah recalled how he looked that first day, fresh from Vietnam, still in uniform as he stepped down from the train. No one knew who he was. His widowed father had moved to the small farm outside of town when Pierre was overseas, and when the older man suddenly died, the son was unable to get home for the funeral. The farm sat vacant, waiting for him until his coming in 1972 at the end of his tour of duty.

Pierre came, intending to stay as he put the war behind him, but not until another military job was completed. The Army asked him to carry out one last task: to accompany, in uniform, the two flag-draped caskets of the town's most recently killed soldiers. And so he did, adding his quiet dignity to that of the dead. He greeted the grieving families at the station, oversaw the loading of the caskets into the waiting hearses. In the next two days he attended both burials, again in uniform, and ceremoniously presented each mother with her folded flag. That was his last military act. He put his uniform away, never to wear it again.

Sarah, herself in her early forties, was childless. She still had her waitress job at the town diner, and she kept busy at home with the flowers and the small herd of Shropshire sheep she insisted they establish on the place right after the marriage. She was a weaver, an artist really, carefully making wool rugs, usually with intricate designs. She sheared the sheep each season, cleaned, carded and spun the wool into yarn. The weaving was done in the slow time of winter. She did well with this work, made money at it, and Pierre was pleased with it. One night in their bed, he told her she had woven him a life.

She loved her flowers as she did her sheep. It seemed to the townspeople that from the earliest days of spring's warmth until the first killing-frost that the little farm's yard was ablaze with blooms. A woolly flower farm she called it: Montreal's Woolly Flower Farm. Two years after their marriage she started naming the different perennial beds. The

Corretta King bed of ebony tulips nestled against the pump house. The Jane Fonda bed grew multicolored irises. The Edith Piaf bed was laid out as the French tricolor; a bed of red, white and blue asters. Her newest bed, of large, sunburst daisies, was the Christa McCauliff bed. She knew that to the younger folk these might not be recognizable names, but when Pierre asked her about them she said they were important to her.

It was nothing big, the names. No one knew about it except Sarah and Pierre. One day he asked why she did not name a bed after a man, so that weekend she put in a small one by the drive. It was for annuals, new, different flowers each year. "That's the Louis Jordan bed," she announced.

THERE WERE NO OTHER BARS in the small town, so the Bullseye, like the town's single church, was given heavy use. The old tavern had tradition, as far as tradition was felt to exist in Northern Wisconsin. In some way the Bullseye was the town. A true social node, it attracted its cadre of daily casual drinkers and was usually busy at night. The noon lunches consisted of nothing more than homemade soups and thick, grilled hamburgers but were very popular. They served to draw a good noontime crowd.

Like the church, the Bullseye was made of red brick. It was two-storied with a flat, tarred roof from which rose the anchored chimney. A satellite dish sat, unnoticed from the street, beside the chimney. Two round parapets at each of the front corners topped the face of the structure. Just above the narrow, tall, second-floor, front windows was an inlaid sandstone block: a profile of a bull's head with a large peering eye that looked down upon the town, had been sculpted out of light tan stone. Below the head was the date: 1883. At ground level, were the usual glass windows that, except for the central doorway with its transom, nearly took up the entire street-side wall. Above the door, projecting out over the sidewalk, was a metal sign with an image of the bull and the tavern's name. The building had not been significantly altered, inside or out, since it was built.

Society does not know its swampers. They do their work quietly, usually out of sight, and are given little thought. In Pierre's case, the townspeople struggled with his tavern cleaning work, to look the other way, to pretend to ignore it. He was the sander at the mill, and was Sarah's man. That is how they knew him.

This Sunday morning, as usual, after he entered the Bullseye, Pierre propped the side door open to let the smelly, trapped air escape, then paused to study the scene. Among the usual liquor and wine bottles on the back bar was the clutter of packages of peanuts, chips, and common snacks preferred by drinkers. On the near end sat the large glass jars of pickled pigs' feet, oversized dill pickles, turkey gizzards, and peeled, hard-boiled eggs. Small plastic sacks of smoked sausages of numerous sorts hung on their cardboard backings on the bar's other end, but at the very ends of the back bar sat two large shiny black ceramic vases. Their locations and size suggested they were meant to highlight the entire array of foods and bottles. These were the flower vases. This morning their white daisies that had been fresh the week before, were beleaguered, bending in fatigue.

As his eyes found the wilted flowers, Pierre raised the fresh gladiolas to his face and searched for their faint aroma. The scene held him for an instant, eyes closed, flower-faced, at the doorway.

The Bullseye was usually in a state of disarray from the debris of the Saturday-night revelers. Yet today, as on all past Sundays, Pierre was ready to bring the old tavern back to life. He walked behind the bar, took the shiny vases down, and removed the expired daisies. He emptied the discolored water and, after rinsing each jar, filled it with fresh tap water. Quickly trimming the gladiolas and placing them into the jars, he set them back onto the back bar. The flowers' tall spikes stood proudly beside the wooden spires on the bar, and seemed, like those compatriots, to be pointing upward to the heavens. This morning, as often happened, he heard a few bars of the church's organ music drifting down the hill through the open door.

Soon, hot water poured into the stainless steel bar sink. Pierre, sleeves rolled just past his elbows, slipped into a clean, white, starched cotton apron and tied it at his back. He took two newly laundered white towels from the barman's cupboard and placed them next to the sink.

Then he began to wash the collection of soiled glasses left at the bar's end the night before. Most were beer glasses. It might have seemed that the tavern, with its heavy woodwork, brick floor and cathedral-like windows, should have served only wine, but the Bullseye's "wine" was beer. Amber glow. There were a few bottles of high-priced liquor on the back bar, and one or two gallon jugs of wine were kept on hand, but for the majority of the drinkers the drink of choice was beer.

Pierre let each of the glasses soak in the hot water with its sanitizing chemicals for a few moments before he brushed them clean, careful to remove any lipstick some might hold. Then he rinsed them. No drip-dry for Pierre Clairebeaux Montreal. Each glass was dried with a clean towel, then, held up to the morning light from the large east windows as it was searched for spots and streaks. The larger beer pitchers were handled with special care. Like sacred chalices, he cleaned each, rinsed, wiped and carefully placed them back on their shelf behind the bar.

When the immediate matters of flowers and glassware were seen to, Pierre stepped out from behind the bar to look it over. The vases were in place, and each glass and pitcher was on its shelf, clean and pure, ready for another week. The bar cloths had been snapped out and carefully folded lengthwise, then hung on their racks, the day's new sunlight drying them. The bar's mirrored back wall reflected the day's light back into the barroom, illuminating the area with its natural, golden color.

Next he turned his attention to the bar itself. Mahogany. Its deep maroon color had darkened with age, rubbed shiny by years of flannel-covered elbows and forearms. It had a dignified air, like the walls and wood furnishings of a well-kept captain's cabin on an ancient schooner. This wood, its exotic origins lost in the passage of time, had been cut in steamy tropical forests in the mid-1800s, then carried by ocean ships to

America and finally by a princely steam locomotive to Northern Wisconsin. Normally out of place in this land of cedar, balsam and aspen, this mahogany seemed to adjust to its fate in the Bullseye. Altar-like, it commanded one's attention.

The top of the bar needed no care, but Pierre wiped down the front, where the shoes and boots of customers sometimes left marks. He buffed its entire length and after finishing, straightened up to gaze at its shine. The front was made from eight pieces of wood—four large squares, one in each corner, that were separated by four other, narrower ones. The four corner squares had a swirled grain pattern that made them stand apart from the narrower strips. These were straight-grained, and each one came to a point in the bar's center. Together they formed a mahogany cross on the bar's front.

Pierre next approached the brass rails that ornamented the bar. His specialty was this brass. He was fascinated by its golden brilliance. He examined the foot rail for a moment, then, quickly stepped out to the Chevrolet. He returned with a homemade wooden box—it was a simple box with a dowel running its length for a handle—and in it were buffing cloths and tin cans of cleansers and polishes. These were special supplies that he took back home each Sunday. Unlike the other cleaning supplies, they did not stay in the tavern's maintenance closet by the basement stairway.

He set to work on his knees at the west end of the foot rail, dabbing on polish before rising to go to the closet and returning with a small electric buffer that he plugged into a wall receptacle. As he buffed the rail, the sun's rays exploded on it, but as he worked his way to the center of the bar he was stopped by a large area of dark water, mostly beer, with, he thought, a hint of urine in it. "Pigs, damn pigs!" he muttered as he rose to bring a mop and bucket to quickly swab it up. This area was particularly littered with cigarette butts and other unidentified debris. Usually flattened on the floor beneath the customers' feet, the butts sometimes caught in the shallow mortared spaces between the floor's bricks and he had to pick them up with his fingers. Pierre often found coins, sometimes even paper bills, ground into the floor's residue. Once he found a tarnished wedding ring, small, for a woman's finger. Sometimes he felt he did not want to examine the mess, almost afraid of what he might recognize.

After the brass was polished to his satisfaction he carried his box of cloths and cleansers back to the Chevrolet. Just after closing the car's trunk he heard the church organ again, this time more loudly, with feeling. It caused him to glance up to the church where the street before it was lined with worshippers' vehicles.

Pierre returned to clean the booths, tables and chairs. Each of the dark booths along the west wall was quickly wiped down and swept out. More butts, spent cigarette packages, stray potato chips, popcorn and other scraps were swept out and left in a row along the edge of the main floor like a line of debris pushed up on a sandy beach. This trash, like the dirtied glassware and the sickly stale air that greeted Pierre upon opening the tavern's door earlier, might have been viewed as the excreta from another Saturday night rite—a weekly, ritual purging.

This morning, throughout his work, except for the exclamation about the nature of pigs, Pierre was generally quiet. He did not turn on the stereo or TV for companionship. He labored by himself, in his own silence. He paused now and then to look at the room, the bar, the sunlit windows, the front door, and, as always, he waited for the Sunday morning train, the 10:47, to pass through on its way from Milwaukee to Rhinelander and on to Duluth, Fargo, and Seattle. As the time drew close, he kept an eye on the Leinenkugel's clock on the west wall, then with only seconds left, stepped to the side door and peered out at the train. He looked intently at any faces he could see in the fleeting windows. Rarely did he miss standing in the doorway to watch the train.

He thought about things, events, people, and meaning. Sometimes his mind took him far from the Bullseye, from the town and farm. He often recalled the street cleaners in Vietnam, how they almost noiselessly and steadily did their work, day after day. He remembered how he used to marvel at these workers who carried on almost serenely, while their country was exploding around them. He saw how the rest of society rushed by, seemingly paying them no heed.

Pierre knew there was no Swamper's Hall of Fame. Perhaps that is why he was so quiet. People did not complain about that, although his silence, coupled with his steady gaze, could at times, become a bit unnerving. No, the townspeople did not criticize him even when he quietly refused their offer to join the American Legion post and then the church on the hill. That fall, when he settled into the farmhouse, they came to him and he gently declined. So the people seemed to say, "Let him be. He is a veteran who has been to war. Maybe that is enough."

Few people asked him about his Sunday morning work. Sarah seemed to understand. She was happy her flowers were enjoyed and shared with others, and she appreciated how Pierre took pride in his work.

He did not go to the Bullseye when it was open for business. He went only on Sunday morning to set it right. One year, at Christmas, he was asked to bring in a large balsam from the farm's woodlot. People admired its beauty and symmetry and it became an institution: The Montreal Tree. So each season he and Sarah chose a tree, cut it and transported it to town atop the Chevrolet. They set it up but did not trim it. It was decorated by others, the same people who put up the other seasons' things in the bar: decorations like the Easter egg bush, the cardboard cutouts of Valentine's hearts and cupids, pumpkins and black cats, and St. Patrick Day hats and clay pipes.

At eleven thirty, Pierre finished wiping out the restrooms and pushed the mop and its wheeled bucket along the narrow hallway behind the bar to the main floor. Each Sunday the last task was to mop the floor. The sun was now higher in the heavens, and its rays angled down sharply, entered the windows, met the colorful neon beer signs and exploded into the room. He enjoyed this time, this last chore on these sunlit Sundays. Cloudy days had a different charm. Their allure came from the subdued light, its effect giving the old tavern a comfortable calmness, as if it were a dimly lit cavern.

The mopping took time—the wringing of the mop, the changing of the water—for he wanted the brick floor to sparkle and radiate the colored light from the windows and the bar's large mirror where the wooden spires and gladiolas rose. As he swung the mop over the bricks, the brass ring at his hip with its musical keys rang in cadence with the mop head's movement. Sometimes a light whistle came from Pierre's puckered lips, joining the keys in song.

Then, just about noon, it was finished. The mop and bucket were put away, the chairs quickly lifted off the tables and placed back onto the floor. As he came to the side door, his body and mind loose, his torso a bit sweaty, with just a bit of fatigue, he reached to the light switches and flicked them off. Then, even more, the sunlight took on a bright, but still soft, golden tone.

Pierre stood in the doorway one last time, the hilltop church bell ringing from across town as the worshippers stepped outdoors. He saw them in their Sunday finery, filing from church and moving to their cars. He turned back to the Bullseye and felt the overall effect. It was led by the amber glow that filled the large room, giving it a pristine appearance. The usual odors of stale beer and exhaled tobacco smoke were gone, replaced at that moment by a soft, fresh and mineral-sweet aroma of the still moist brick floor. It was a time Pierre cherished, caught in a few moments while he paused, hand on doorknob, to glance back at the effect of his labor. He inhaled deeply, filling his lungs. Like a temple, the tavern, with its altar-like mahogany bar, its brass, sparkling glassware and tawny liquor bottles was ready for the new week.

As the parishioners' vehicles left the church's graveled parking lot, Pierre pulled the door shut, locked it and stepped to the Chevrolet. Starting the engine, he turned the wheel, came around the block to the main street and drove up the hill, eastward, back to Sarah and the farm.

❧ Reservation ❧

ക 15 ര

Firsts

Conversations about before their arrival,
about who had lived there before were
never given audience—

—David Treuer, 1995

HE HILL WAS THE HIGHPOINT on the farm. Red granite outcroppings marked it, made it visible from a mile or more. Yet it was not a high hill. It was simply a rise in the land too steep to plow—too dangerous to maneuver machinery over—so it was left alone. Only the dairy herd came to it with any regularity when the black-and-white Holsteins tore at its grasses each spring and sought shelter under its few remaining red oaks in summer storms.

Late in July and sometimes in August, the ponderous cows would gather at the little slough-like pond that lay just below the hill. They waded out into the dark muck, amongst the cattails, seeking the coolness offered by the remaining water. Sometimes a gangly shypoke (an American bittern) joined them. The silvery minnows that managed to survive in the small pond offered the bird meager fare.

121

The family that farmed the 240 acres no longer celebrated the hill with its tiny water source. They knew water bubbled up into the pond from a natural spring, and they knew the story of how, back in the 1850s when their immigrant ancestor, Henry Muller, cleared the land, that he and his wife, Madeline, used the pond as their water source. They knew also of the dusty wooden box, no larger than a shoebox, up in the house's attic. They knew, or at least the older members of the family knew, that the box held a few handfuls of brown ceramic potsherds collected by Grandma Muller, it was said, from beside the pond. Nondescript, dull brown with only a hint of faded vermilion linear designs on a few, the shards were appealing enough to the woman to pick them up, to examine them in her callused, weather-hardened hands, and finally, to bring them down to the house.

So the hill and its pond played an important role in the lives of these early settlers, but that was during the years before they dug a well down by the home site. Sometime after the digging of the well, when the farm was showing an acceptable return each season, the family left the pond to the cattle, except to use it for one more purpose: the farm dump. It was considered wasteland, a part of the farm that would have been tiled if not for the difficulty of the constancy of the spring's flow. The digging for the laying of the tile, the work and expense, it was concluded, would have been too much. The acreage was enough without the effort to make the pond's portion of it cultivable.

All farms in that part of Wisconsin had their dumps. Household trash, the metal refuse from the machine shed, rusty rolls of old fencing—anything that could not burn or quickly decay was hauled out to the slough and dumped. A few large gray crumbling bones were sometimes brought up by the frost beside the pond. These were from earlier farm horses and cattle that perished in the days before the rendering plant's greasy, smelly truck plied the region's farms for dead and down stock.

Now, with the national concern for the environment and with local efforts at recycling reusable materials, the family no longer discarded its metal, glass, plastic and other hard materials in the slough. It was left to the cattle, this "swamp" as it was beginning to be called. Even though now and then a cow was injured by a length of barbed wire or a piece of broken glass at the slough, the cows were left to use it, to claim the pond and hill as theirs. These days, only a few lengths of rusty tin rain gutters and several other unidentifiable metal objects protruded from the water at one end of the slough. The rest of the debris, like the pond itself, was gone, out of sight and memory, forgotten by the family.

LAST MAY, DURING HIS FOURTEENTH YEAR, Travis Muller, a great-great grandson of Henry and Madeline, was walking the newly worked field that lay along the eastern side of the granite outcropping when he found the lance point. Bending to pick it up from the dusty earth, the boy instantly saw its craftsmanship and was momentarily struck by it. Rose colored, with a few cream striations running diagonally from upper left to lower right, it told of a stone-knapper's careful selection of his material. Made of chert, it had the small flake scars along its edges from its tip to the concave base. On each side carefully placed flutes narrowed the last half-inch of the base, making room for the hardwood shaft.

Travis stood for a few moments, the lance point in his left hand, as he studied it, rubbing it clean with his thumb. He tested its sharpness with the index finger of his right hand and was impressed with its edge. Soon it was placed into a side pants pocket as he continued his walk up to the oaks. The lance point, the first he ever found, would be shown to the family later.

It was a Sunday afternoon, and the rest of the family was in the house, lazily relaxing in the living room with the television. Major league baseball was on but no one seemed to actually be watching the game. A large, heavy dinner had slowed them, and some dozed on the overstuffed couch and recliner as the television set droned on, inning after inning. Travis's two older brothers, stuffed with the huge meal prepared by their mother, lay like beached whales, asleep on the carpeted floor, their heaviness due in part to the previous night's activities at the nearby town's dancehall. Loud polka music, the effects of cold beer and the playful laughter of young women were still with them. Even Betty, Travis's young sister, who often joined him on these walks, had stayed behind, preferring to rest.

The Muller family was well known in the county. Some members had shown livestock at the county fair each September for years. Ribbons were won; their display cases in the house's dining room overflowed, but over the years it wasn't just the blocky diary cattle that took prizes. The fields claimed their share as well. If a season's corn, oats, and alfalfa crops were especially good, samples were sometimes entered into competition. The hybrid corn, heavy oat kernels, and leafy, tender alfalfa hay won their shares of prizes, too.

Two years ago, Travis's mother, Sylvia, entered some of her craftwork, winning a blue ribbon for a patchwork quilt, its red, white and blue colors designed as the American flag. It caught the eye of the judges and was selected as first runner-up for the Best of Show Award. A large cotton wall-hanging done with exquisitely executed needlework took the more coveted, Best of Show prize. It held the somber black and white Prisoner of War-Missing in Action flag, calling attention to soldiers still unaccounted for in one of the nation's latest wars.

The Muller farm was a Century Farm, designated as such by state authorities for having been worked by the same family for over 100 years. These prestigious farms were decreasing in number as corporate farming became more and more evident. A black-and-white sign out at the township road by the driveway told passersby of the Century Farm designation.

That Sunday in May when Travis wanted more than the companionship of the family, he restlessly went to the back hall and put on his blue denim work jacket, his faded New York Yankees baseball cap, and strolled outdoors through the farmyard. Tall for his fourteen years, the boy was beginning to fill out in the upper torso. His dark-brown hair, not covered by the cap, was visible around his temples, ears and at the back of his head. It was cut short, its color being challenged by the boy's darkening skin. With the coming of spring a deep suntan was beginning to spread across his otherwise light face.

The current farm dog, a collie and German shepherd mix, ambled beside him, watching his every move, hoping, it seemed, to be part of whatever the boy was up to. After walking through the yard, he followed a pathway that started behind the large, red hip-roofed dairy barn. This pleased the dog, for it enjoyed an opportunity for a romp in the far pasture. It ran ahead of Travis as they moved along the grassy lane. They were on the narrow, fenced walkway that allowed the cattle to move between the barn and the pasture. It began at the barn's back door and stretched out through the cleared fields. The family felt that Great-Grandfather Muller had planned its direction to the distant pastures, and while that is what actually happened, it was not the complete story.

The pathway was in the wooded land when the first Mullers bought the acreage back in the 1850s. It was simply a footpath through the forest that led to the granite hill and the pond. Over the years it was forgotten. Its southern portion, the part that ran along the low roll of the land, where the farm had been cleared of trees, brush and stumps over one hundred years before, and planted to corn, oats, wheat, or alfalfa, was almost obliterated. No one seemed to notice it anymore for it was only a thin pencil line of lighter soil running from the southern fenced boundary of the farm to where the farmyard stood.

The footpath's northernmost portion was a bit more visible, but also went unmentioned. It began only about a hundred feet beyond the barnyard as it meandered over the northern fields, following the high ground again, leaving its light pencil line visible only when the fields were plowed, or smoothed in preparation for planting. Once the crops came up, it was lost in the green foliage, but even in those short times when the fields were bare, only the thoughtful eye noted it.

For years and years the barbed fence line with its gray, weathered cedar posts bisected the path, pulling the onlooker's line of sight along the east-west run of the cultivated fields, away from the diagonal pencil line that followed the flow of the land itself. The plow's furrows ignored this natural flow, for the rises and falls of the fields were hardly noticeable and not a factor in matters of spring runoffs, or severe summer rainstorms. There was no fear of erosion.

It was this thin light pencil line that caused Travis to pause that spring Sunday, to spread the two middle strands of barbed wire, bend down and carefully step through, first one leg, then the other. Perhaps it was the gentleness of the day, the slow cool wind from the east, the lilting call of a meadowlark standing out in the field, barely visible on the brown earth. For whatever cause, if there even was one, the boy walked slowly along the ancient pathway, cutting diagonally across the field, a pathway that would lead him to the spring on the granite hill. Perhaps he was unknowingly following the land itself, its silent flowing movement to the hilltop.

It was in this field, on the remnant of this ancient footpath, that he found the lance point. It laid completely exposed, atop the recently cultivated soil, where it must have been worked up, after it was last used, long, long ago.

After passing over the rest of the tilled field and stepping through the last fence, Travis was at the pond. He turned to the right, circumnavigating the muddy edges pockmarked with the double-toed hoof prints of the ungulate Holsteins. Coming up on the northern side of the waterhole, he slowly moved past the large oaks, their deep-red spring leaves beginning to enlarge and turn to a bright, almost fluorescent green, before assuming the deeper green of summer.

Travis found the granite outcroppings and soon was resting on his favorite place, leaning back in an upright, seated position, his back against the wall of crumbling stone. The dog sat beside him. The boy thought of this little ledge as his spot, his place. Once the constant work of summer arrived, he would have little time to spend here, but now, in late spring, he came often. It was pleasant to look down on the farm as it unfolded to the east. The farmstead, nestled in its grove of trees facing the blacktop township road, had its back to the hill, so it was as if the boy was afforded a seat to observe the farm, to watch and contemplate its being, while the farmstead's attention was focused in the other direction, to the road and to the town, seven miles distant.

This Sunday was a holiday: Memorial Day, and the family attended church services in town where the small Lutheran church was nearly filled. After the services most of the congregation walked to the adjacent cemetery and observed the ceremony put on by the Veterans of Foreign Wars; the laying of the black plastic wreath at the large stone monument near the cemetery's entrance, the short speech given by the VFW post commander, and even a talk on patriotism offered by the chairwoman of the village council. The local high school band played the brassy national anthem, followed by the VFW honor guard's six-gun salute, and finally by the lone trumpeter hidden at the rear of the cemetery, playing taps behind a large oak tree.

After the ceremony, upon returning home, Sylvia put the finishing touches on the roast turkey dinner she had started earlier that morning. The dinner was the usual large Sunday kind, complete with mashed potatoes and light gravy, at least two types of vegetables, homemade white bread and dessert.

Today, two large, double-crusted apple pies, made from the last of the basement's apples, was the dessert. In late spring Sylvia liked to clear the fruit cellar of anything left from the previous season; a ritual cleansing that readied it for the new year's produce. It was after the pie was served, and the white, creamy vanilla ice cream had been scooped onto each person's wedge that Travis's father gave the second prayer of the meal. This was a family custom, this recitation of two prayers. The opening prayer before the main course was the usual kind, offering thanks for the food. The second prayer was different. It was well known to the family, since it was given at almost all holiday meals, but it was especially important at the big ones like Easter, Thanksgiving and

127

Christmas. Memorial Day was right up there in importance, and the Muller family had a tradition of honoring it.

So they knew what would be said, how all would bow their heads, fold their hands in their laps and listen as Travis's father offered thanks. There were thanks, of course, for all those who had gone to war, and especially for those who did not return. And since it was spring, recognition of this promising time of year was always made. Spring on the farm was felt by the family as a time of joy and expectation. The natural world was coming alive again. The fields were waiting.

Most importantly during this second prayer, as always, gratitude was offered to the ancestors, to that pioneering set of settlers in the last century who came to America and built the farm, who were the first to make it a home, to clear the wilderness away and plow the earth, turning it into fields. Travis's father was sincere in his gratitude to these people who, he was careful to remind his children, were the first ones. They had given so much so those who followed could have an easier and better life.

THE EXTRAVAGANT DINNER, the prayers, and the ceremony in town with its show of colors and sounds still filled the boy's mind as he relaxed on the rock outcropping. He wondered if he too, would wear a military uniform someday. His father and grandfather both had, and there were all those cousins and uncles who served. A few women had also gone to war—his great-aunt Phyllis in the Women's Air Corps in World War II and even a distant cousin who was a nurse in Vietnam.

Travis's father was a veteran of the Korean War. The youngsters were proud of this and wanted him to talk about his time overseas but through the years they were told very little. Instead their father preferred to talk of Uncle Jim, who had been in New Guinea in World War II and later was wounded in Manila. It seemed Uncle Jim was the real war hero in the family, but the children heard more of the ancestors who built the farm than about family members who went to war. They were familiar with how Grandpa and Grandma Muller struggled to keep the farm going during the Depression of the 1930s.

When they were younger, war was a preoccupation for the boys. Their mock battles, usually fought in and around the cavernous barn, sometimes pitted the Americans against the Vietnamese, and even the North Koreans, but most of their battles were fought "Rambo style." Their enemy was hiding in the imaginary jungles that magically spread through the farmyard. The boys used plastic AK-40s and Russian-styled automatic rifles. The enemy's identity was never really clear. It was not important. With time these wars moved to the high school basketball courts, football, and baseball fields where their opponents were from distant towns and farms.

Once, at the supper table, one of the boys asked how many wars the family had seen.

"World War I, II, Korea, Vietnam—" their mother began to answer.

"Don't forget San Juan Hill, Ma," one of the older boys said.

"Well, if you're going back that far we have to start with 1776," Sylvia went on. "Then there was the Civil War—and what about when we invaded Honduras? I suppose we'd have to count that too."

"Was Korea really a war, Dad?" Travis asked, turning to his father across the table. "Isn't it called a police action?"

"Well, we used to call it the forgotten war, but now we have the monument," his father said.

"We should go see that monument someday," an older brother interjected. "Where is it—Washington, D.C.?"

"So now we have no forgotten wars?" Travis asked his parents.

"I guess that's right," said his father. "We must have monuments for nearly all of them by now."

"War, war, war. Why all the monuments to war? Why not a monument for peace?" Heads turned to Betty, Travis's ten-year-old sister.

"What would that be? A big white dove?" an older brother said, deprecatingly. "Dahhh—" he concluded, giving the girl the current expression for stupidity.

"Been there. Done that," another brother said. "There's a monument of a big white dove in Paris. It's for world peace."

"Not Paris—it's in Switzerland, stupid," offered the other older brother.

"You're both wrong. It's a peace garden, and it's in North Dakota," Betty countered.

THE ROSE-COLORED LANCE POINT raised no eyebrows when Travis returned to the house from the hill. Even Betty, who at least took it into her hand to examine it, soon set it back down onto the shelf by the kitchen window were it lay in the sunlight behind the potted African violets. In a week or so, when dusting, Travis's mother placed it into the shoebox in the back hall cabinet with the accumulation of other oddities, curios, and misplaced small objects that made their way into the house. The box held the bolts, screws and nails sometimes left in pockets she discovered when doing the laundry.

When placing the lid onto the cardboard shoebox and slipping it back onto the cabinet shelf, Sylvia called to mind, although fleetingly, the older wooden box up in the house's dusty attic, the box holding the smooth ceramic potshards put away by Henry Muller's wife, Madeline. Perhaps it was where the stone point belonged, she thought, and perhaps she would take it up there someday.

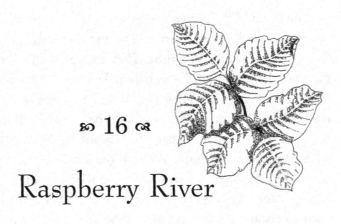

∞ 16 ∞

Raspberry River

*I finally realized that I needed to become
part of the land again, and regain my roots
and my identity.*

—Wub-e-ke-niew, 1995

RANDMA ATTIKOOSH SAID WE were Water People. So we must
be fish clan. I don't know. Maybe we *are* Sturgeon like she said.
Maybe she heard it when she was young. But me, I think I'm
related to poison ivy. There aren't supposed to be any plant *dodems* for
the Ojibwe—at least the elders say all our clans were named for animals—so I guess I'm wrong, but I must be related to the ivy because I'm
not allergic to it. I can walk through it, touch it, handle it with my bare
hands, and never catch it. That makes us kin. Ever since I can remember,
the ivy and I have gotten along.

They tell the story of camping at Raspberry River. I must have
been one year old. Auntie Stell says I tumbled down that bank that was
full of it. She was sure I drowned because she had to come around by
the path and by the time she pulled me out I went down three times.

One more and I'd a'been a goner, she said. No, she wasn't going to come down that bank. She ran around by the footpath.

That was the first time. They thought I didn't catch it because of the river. Even though I was bare naked when I fell into that poison ivy patch I didn't get it. They said it was the *nibi*—the river's water that washed it off—that clear water. And they said it was the slime, too—the sturgeon slime. That's what they meant by Water People. The water takes care of us, they said. We're *of* the water, we're *Nibi People*.

Auntie Stell says sturgeon used to spawn in the river, right by the campground. They'd come up in the shallows and one spring her dad tried to spear one, but couldn't. She said it was wrong for him to try because those big fish are our relatives, but he tried anyway, and when the spear glanced off he jumped in to hogtie that big fish, but it got away. Its slime was so thick his arms kept slipping off. The fish escaped to deep water and made it back to the lake.

That's what Auntie Stell meant. My slime must have kept that ivy from stinging me. Sturgeon slime protected me. That's how the Old People used to think. "We're connected," they said. "All Water People are, but only we sturgeon have the slime."

RASPBERRY RIVER IS OUR RIVER. It's the last place on The Rez that is all tribal land. The river runs only through tribal land. No whites own property along its banks. It's the last pristine drainage on the entire reservation. It's five miles long and nowhere along its reach has any development taken place, so the water is ours. Rain and snow fall on that Indian land and drain to the river, then, finally to Lake Superior. It feels good just to think about this. Nibi— clear, cold and sweet. It's still ours.

I DIDN'T REALLY KNOW ABOUT BAD MEDICINE until I got back from Vietnam. Both Auntie Stell and my ma were gone by then. I was drinking a lot, not thinking much about anything. It wasn't very good then.

I was too heavy, sloppy even. I know people say I am tall and that tall men can carry their weight, but I was beyond the acceptable limit. Now I watch it, take care of myself.

But before, my jobs came and went. Labor jobs. I picked apples, took different low paying jobs for the tribe, but at least they kept me going. But they were grant money; soft money that eventually ran out. I even had a job on the ferry for a while, showing the people where to park their cars. It was good out on the water on those trips. After the boat was loaded there was nothing for me to do so I'd stand way out in the bow during the crossing, looking down at the water, watching how it opened to let us enter—let us ride it over to the island.

I liked the sound of the waves breaking away from the boat, liked the way they looked—transparent-like. I could see into them. And I liked the smell. Clean, cold, fresh water smells good. That's when I started to think about Auntie Stell, Ma, an' dem. Now I see it was like that water was trying to tell me something.

But the drinking and the screwing kept on. Maybe the women liked to think they were lying with a war hero. I don't know, but those years were filled with booze and women. Then one day it hit me. I was walking down the sidewalk in town—tourists were all over. Suddenly I realized they were moving away from me. They'd see me coming, and step aside, sometimes even cross the street to the other sidewalk. What the hell. I sobered up, started going to the sweats.

I GOT HIS PHONE NUMBER from Bixie Cadotte. He said he knew him well, said that he could help me. So one day I called. He said to come down on Saturday, said he was holding an open sweat that night. When I drove into his yard I didn't see any other cars. As it turned out we were the only one's in the lodge—just me and this old man.

After, when we sat outside in his back yard, he started telling me things. I kept the little fire going while he talked. His wife brought out some coffee and a few sandwiches. "There really is no bad medicine," he started.

"Some people say you Water People are bad medicine, but that's not true. There are some powerful spirits that live in waters, in the rivers and lakes. There is a spirit in there that can rival the Thunderbirds, and that's power.

"Most things and places have power. That's just the way it is. It's how we use that power that is important. If we don't use it at all, don't accept it, we have trouble. If we use it too much, or if we use it the wrong way, we're in trouble, too. Spirits are good. We have to understand that. We have to learn how to accept and use all that power."

THINGS STARTED TO SETTLE DOWN after that. The tribe gave me a job working with the vets, even sent me to workshops and conferences. Last fall they let me take some classes over at the college. I like to go over there, even though it's tough, reading all those books.

Sometimes I have to get away from them, so I drive out to Raspberry, usually on weekends. Yesterday I drove out and did a little duck hunting, but mostly I just wanted to be on the river. That old dented canoe is still stashed in the cattails where Grandpa Attikoosh used to have his shack. I pushed off, lay my shotgun down at my feet and never picked it up until I came back. Once out on the water the river just took over.

The colored leaves were nice to look at. I slowly paddled the mile to the lake, went out into the bay, made a big loop and came back up the river. A few sailboats were in the bay and I heard some kayakers on the beach, saw them around a little campfire, eating and laughing.

Coming back upstream I saw that the bank of poison ivy was a deep red, like the ripe Macintoshes in the orchards south of the reservation, toward town. It was downright beautiful. I was surprised to see the patch was still there after all these years, but why shouldn't it have been there?—it's the same river, the same bank, the same place, even after thirty-some years.

After stashing the canoe back in the cattails and putting the gun in the car I walked through the campground and out to the beach. It's always good to walk across that wooden walkway through the swamp, even though its low places sometimes give me wet feet. Last evening I noticed how the fly-catching pitcher plants have turned, like the ivy and apples, a deep red, their summer's work over. The tiny orchid plants that bloom in late spring were getting ready for winter, too. They were dropping some of their leaves.

By the time I got to the long sand beach the kayakers had left. Their little fire was covered with sand, and I was pleased that no bottles, cans or other garbage was left lying around. Reaching the end of the beach I turned to come back to the boardwalk. Five large sailboats were in the bay, some already anchored for the night. I heard the voices of the people out there, saw a few tending small charcoal grills topside. It must be nice to have such a sailboat, to escape the city for a weekend, to anchor in this untouched bay. It must be nice to grill steaks and to watch the sunset from the calm water.

RASPBERRY VILLAGE?" I SAID. "Really?"

"Yes," Bixie was saying. "People used to live out there in the late 1800s. You can see it written on some of the early census papers. Where it says 'Place of Birth,' Raspberry Village is sometimes written in."

I was in Bixie's trailer home, having coffee, watching Monday Night Football. His wife was at Bingo so we had the trailer to ourselves. Bixie, his large belly like a big bubble under his shirt, lay back in his recliner, watching the game. At the quarters he rose to go to the kitchen for more Pepsi.

"My pa used to talk about it. He remembered it from when he was little. He said there was quite a village out there. Some had tarpaper wigwams, some small log houses, and others just small, square, flat-topped tarpaper shacks. It was the river and lake that held them. They were fishermen—fishing just about all year long. Even in winter they'd go out into the channel to bob through the ice for the big lakers. Now-a-days we're told not to eat those big lake trout because of the heavy metal, but back then they were good."

"Where was it?" I asked. "Right along the river or out by the beach?"

"He said it was mostly back by the river, I guess where the campground is now. But he talked about a cemetery, somewhere closer to the beach. I guess he witnessed a few of the last burials, at least he said something once, about the priest coming across that old boardwalk, falling into the swamp, getting all wet and being so mad that he cut the burial ceremony real short. He yelled at the people for not keeping the walkway in better shape."

"The poor father—" I chuckled.

"Hell," Bixie laughed. "The poor guy that was buried. I hope he got all of the last rites that he was supposed to."

Later that week, I met Father Bill at the grocery. His large body dwarfed the cart he was pushing. I asked him if he knew about an old cemetery out at Raspberry. He stopped and turned his red, flushed cheeks to me, then said he didn't but that he would take a quick check through some of the early burial records in the church basement in town. Thursday evening he phoned, saying he had something. I drove in to see.

When he let me in he said to come into the kitchen, that he was cutting a pizza just taken out of the microwave. I joined him at the table and we ate while studying the old records. "It must have been in use before the mid-1800s," the priest said, looking down at the black leather-bound ledger. "See here?" he went on. "This says a person named Abel Morrison was administered the rites of Christian burial in the 'Old Pagan Cemetery' at Raspberry Village. That was in 1867."

"Where do you think it was—the old burial ground?" I asked, bending to read the faded handwriting.

"I don't have any idea," said Father Bill, wiping his lips and chin with a paper napkin, his first two tall fingers of his right hand stained a deep yellow-to-brown. "I'll do some more looking downstairs. Maybe I can find something. I'll let you know."

Driving my dusty pickup truck back to the rez, I took pleasure in seeing the deep blue of Lake Superior through the colorful trees. I thought about Abel Morrison, how he must have converted, then died out at Raspberry and was buried by the lake. It seemed a good resting place. Then I thought about the word, pagan. I recalled how Bixie said it was an old word that meant anybody whose religion wasn't one of the big world religions. "Pagan," I said aloud in the truck. "Pagan." A pagan cemetery, I thought. I imagined ceremonies for pagans buried by Lake Superior back in the mid-1800s, the drumming, the singing, the tobacco. The word, pagan, no longer carried the humorous, negative meaning it was given when I was in grade and high school in town. Pagans were people, I told myself. Hey, I thought, Bixie is a pagan. I'm a pagan. "Pagan" was starting to have a nice ring, a defiant, strong, powerful sound to it.

FATHER BILL CALLED ONE EVENING the following week. He apologized for taking so long to get back to me, then said he found an old sketch of where the burial ground was. I drove to town immediately.

"From the looks of this, I'd say it was about a few hundred feet or so from the beach, way down on the southern end somewhere. This shows the river's mouth right here," he pointed to a place on the paper showing the north end of the beach, "and the cemetery should be way down here, somewhere far to the south." Looking up from the old paper, the priest asked, "Does that help you?"

"Oh, ya," I said excitedly. "This is great. I think I'll go out on Saturday for a look-see. Thanks."

"Let me know what you find. I should really go out there and sprinkle some holy water around if you come up with something. We should probably put up a cross, too."

"Okay," I answered, turning away to hide the smile that suddenly came across my face. "I'll call you."

On Saturday I stopped at Bixie's place. He gladly came along.

At first we thought it was too late, that the rising and falling of the lake level over the years had obliterated any marks of the graves. The place inked on the old church paper made it clear that it was an open area, not covered with trees, because the woods was distant from the lake and swamp. We knew that an open grassy patch of high ground lay between the ridge of the old beach line the furthest from the lake. This grassy area was higher than the swamp and never, we thought, flooded during the spring runoff. It was protected from the lake by the high ridge that kept even the highest lake levels out.

And it was in the grassy area that we finally found the tell-tale depressions that told of sunken graves. One had a short piece of metal sticking out at one end, only an inch or two. It was green, like old copper. Bixie tugged at it and found an early cross that must have stood at the grave's head.

"Wah," he uttered when it easily slid out of the ground. "Look at this." He held it out to me.

"Hammered copper," I said. "I wonder if it's from Michigan. Maybe it came over from Europe," I went on, looking for some mark.

It told of change going on over one hundred years ago. It told of the invasion.

"Today this is a collector's item. Someone will steal it for sure," Bixie said. "We should bury it, at least cover it up with dirt. Maybe the family of this person felt strongly about it."

Using the long end of the cross as a spade he carefully scratched a hole on the top of the grave, big enough and deep enough to safely hide the cross, then laid it into its own grave, stepped it down deeper into the loose soil, and with a toe spread the disturbed ground over it.

We quietly walked the site, checking what appeared to be gravesites. For several minutes no one spoke. Only the slow, but clearly heard, lap of the lake's small waves onto the sandy beach was audible. And the wind. The gentle lake wind was always with us.

Suddenly Bixie broke the silence as he shouted for me to come to see what he found. The rectangular outline of wooden boards framing a grave was visible at ground level. Mostly covered with earth and grass, the shiny, gray color of the weather-hardened wood made the boards look like clean pieces of driftwood, glistening in the sun.

The top's gone," Bixie said. "This place must have been full of grave houses." Then, standing before the grave, looking down at it, he reached to his left shirt pocket, pulled out his pack of cigarettes, tapped one out, and handed it to me. Then he quietly said, "When I die I want you to build one of these for me." I readily took the cigarette, placing it into my side jacket pocket.

THE SPIRIT NEEDS HELP ON ITS TRIP. It needs food and good thoughts. It needs tobacco. When it crosses the river the log bridge can turn and twist like a big snake, like a troubled serpent. The weak and unfortunate sometimes fall, but the others, with the help of the living, make it to the other side. There they are reunited with those who went before, and it is there that they wait for us to join them.

SURROUNDED BY BULRUSHES on the lakeside and by cattails on the swamp side, the flat, high grassy circular opening lay hidden from both the swamp and lake. It surprised us when we came upon it. Bixie, I suspect, was a bit embarrassed that he had not checked out the cemetery's existence all these years. The location, way down at the far southern end of the beach was probably why it laid there undetected for so long. No one, really, ventured that far, and if they did, when reaching the end of the beach, they turned around and walked back. Part of its anonymity was due to how, in the old times, a cemetery was not a place you frequented. Burial sites were often left alone, to be claimed by the workings of the *manitog*.

But there was more to our surprise than simply locating the pagan burial ground. When immediately upon coming over the high ridge, and we found a small, narrow footpath through the tall wall of bulrushes, I recall how Bixie, who was ahead, said, "A game trail," but when we broke through the last of the green plants, we were met with a dumping ground. Along the inner edge of the bulrushes and cattails that served as the perimeter of the shorter grass were piles of human feces, most topped with crumpled, white tissue paper. Shit. It was human shit. Piles of shit.

And, along with this unfortunate sight we found small piles of plastic and glass bottles—many of the popular brands of bottled water— and the familiar aluminum beer cans and assorted food containers and wrappers. Refuse, we concluded, dumped from kayakers and sail boaters, from these newest of reservation invaders, now coming by the sea. Seeing themselves as good environmentalists, they must have felt it important not to leave their trash on the beach, so they brought it back here, to the cemetery. We concluded they knew what they were doing, and we wondered about how items as offerings left atop the graves so long ago, might have survived the years, like the weathered grave house boards and copper cross, only to be carried off in these recent times.

Then suddenly, angrily, Bixie raised his head to the sky, his long, black braid hanging straight down in the air behind him, and with closed eyes screamed a long, piercing, frustrated wail. This he followed with the shouted condemnation: "Damn them! Damn them! Now they're shit-ting on our dead!"

And indeed, they were. It seemed that the slight depressions of the old graves were deemed good places to squat and take care of one's busi-ness, since a few of the depressions had shit and toilet paper in them. For long moments we stood in shocked disbelief, surveying the mess.

Finally, I said, "I guess I can understand the kayakers, but don't the sailboats have johns on them?"

Bixie and I came back on Sunday to remove the cans, bottles and other rubbish. Using black plastic leaf bags, we carried out two nearly full sacks. The desecration from human bodily waste we scraped up and buried back by the cattails.

"Should we put up a 'No Trespassing' sign?" I asked on our last trip out with the bags.

"There're enough of those in the world already," Bixie said, shaking his head. "I'll see the Council about it. Something has to be done. This place is going to be off limits."

"Well," I said, quietly. "There is something I'm going to do, me. Saturday morning. I'll get at it first thing Saturday morning."

THE ROOTS CAME OUT OF THE BANK EASILY. I had counted the graves and knew I needed at least thirty-two plants. That wasn't many. The job was accomplished slowly, with thoughtful care. Using a small garden trowel, I knelt in the patch, and spread the plants carefully, trying not to dislodge the deep red leaves that were beginning to fall off. At the start, when I placed the tobacco down at the foot of the bank, I asked the plants for forgiveness, telling them of the problem, of our need for their help.

With bare hands I carefully removed each plant, trying to keep at least a fistful of damp soil around its length of root. The red clay cooperated, clinging to the roots as I carefully placed each plant into the white plastic bucket. It took four trips. It was good to kneel with the plants, to be amongst them, to feel them press onto my knees. And it was good to feel the brush of their leaves on the skin of my hands and forearms. We're related.

As I knelt again, out beside the beach, I carefully used my trowel to prepare each planting hole. A pinch of tobacco went in first, next the plants were slowly removed from the bucket and lowered into the shallow holes, the damp earth gently pressed firmly around each. Using the empty bucket I carried lake water to the graves and gave each plant enough to set the soil around its roots.

I knew that in spring the plants would be up, their new leaves opening for another year. I knew they would be ready with their powerful medicine. When, at the conclusion of the planting, I bent at the edge of the grassy area to place the closing tobacco offering, I thanked the plants once again, and I wished them well. In a season or two they would cover the area, protecting what lay below. I told them their medicine was strong, that I knew they would use it correctly.

17

Killing Horses

*"Shamans," she said. "That's why the Lord
sent us here, to rescue these poor heathens
from such darkness."*

—the missionary, Hazel Quarrier in *At Play
in the Fields of the Lord*, by Peter Mathiessen, 1963

BILL, JACK SOMMERFIELD WAS OUT TODAY. Wants ya ta work tomorrow. Bill? D'ja hear? Jack Sommerfield was out. Wants ya ta work tomorrow. Needs help with some horses. I forgot ta tell you." With that she returned to the kitchen to finish the dishes.

Bill had quickly dozed off on the couch in the front room after the meal. It was a windy day, and he ached from the wood. "Huh?" he grunted. "Horses? What happened to Solly? He was doin' that."

"Solly's not around. Jack said he left for Chicago. Workin' in Chicago," she said over her shoulder from the sink. "Ya better go," she continued, "that's good money."

"Good money hell," he said, now awake, still lying on his back, elbows pointing up beside his ears, hands linked under his head. "I've always made good money. I'm a workin' fool. That's why ya married me—'member?"

"Wah," she snorted as she wrung the dishcloth to wipe the table. "Ya can cut that wood later. Better grab this job while ya can. He pays good."

"To hell with it. I'm cuttin' wood now. That sap's gonna be movin' soon and den what? Can't run a sugarbush without firewood. Besides, Harry's comin' early tomorrow."

She didn't pursue it. She knew better than to argue when he set his mind to something.

The next morning he rose at dawn. He poured water into the washbasin, splashed his face and quickly shaved while watching himself in the small mirror on the wall. He liked what he saw: the square chin, dark eyes, heavy, black eyebrows. As he quickly combed his dark hair, he felt he was ready for the day.

She heard him moving around in the kitchen, making fire, coffee, and packing his lunch. Lard sandwiches. Bacon grease on her homemade white bread. That was his usual fare when in the woods. Soon she heard Harry's team plod into the yard with the sled scraping on the packed snow. The door slammed and she heard the muffled sounds of the horses' big hooves as they padded out and down the snow-packed dirt road.

For the past several mornings Bill and Harry walked the four miles to the sugarbush, but today Harry wanted to bring a little firewood back. The winter had been harsh, even for Northern Wisconsin, and the piles in his yard were almost depleted. "Hate to burn green wood," he said, "but what can I do?"

When they reached the ridge beside the lake, they turned off the township road and drove the team through the woods about three quarters of a mile on an early logging trail. The sugarbush's woodlot ran along the ridge—a ridge full of white and yellow birch—that stretched for miles parallel to the lake. Lake Superior's ice gleamed through the leafless trees, and, Bill thought, it really did resemble a huge *migiis* shell, the sacred saltwater shell of the Old People.

After securing the horses in the brush windbreak under the large hemlock, the men took their axes and the two-man crosscut saw and headed up the ridge, away from the lake, where they were working for the past several days. Harry had filed the saw the night before, and soon it was biting into the birch, spitting out large, bright bits of clean wood. After several trees were lying on the snow, they set to work with their small cruising axes, limbing them. The music of cold steel biting into hard birch wood resounded like notes bouncing off painted walls in a concert hall, but instead of fancy city concert hall walls, this morning they ricocheted from tree to tree, finally dying away in the cold air of the March skies.

Bill told Harry of Jack Sommerfield and the fox farm job. When they stopped for a drink from the glass water jug Harry began to chuckle. "So, what happened to Solly?" he asked. "Did it get too hot for him?"

"I don't know," Bill replied. "That's tough work, killin' horses."

"Hell," Harry said.

"It's tough," Bill repeated. "Old Jack is no fun to work for. That son-of-a-bitch never did learn how to get along with people. And when he's drinkin', he's no fun to be around. No sir. You'd think as old as he is that he'd have learned something by now."

"He never shouldda married her," Harry continued. "A young woman like that needs a younger man. That's the trouble. He's worried."

"Awh, Solly wouldn't touch her," Bill said. "He'd be scared to."

"Maybe so," Harry replied, "but you never know. She's hungry and damn good lookin' with that long black hair and all. How'd you like to stay on that place all day and not get into town wid'out Old Jack watchin' ya all da time? Solly must'a gotten into somethin' and got out while he could."

"Shit," Bill said.

"They eat horsemeat, ya know," Harry continued, looking at Bill. "Steaks. Big ones. Each Sunday right after church. He makes her cook them. She must be eating it too by now."

"White people eat anything," Bill countered. "That's okay. That's just more venison for me."

144

"Well, look out," Harry said as he used a small whetstone to put an edge back onto his ax. "Just be careful. That old man's nuts. You never know what he'll do."

That evening, before supper, Jack Sommerfield was at the back door. Bill went out and stood in the yard beside the fox farm pickup truck. They talked about the weather, how the sap would be running soon, and how the winter had been hard on most things. Finally they got around to the fox farm and the horses. Bill's gaze lifted from the yard when Jack brought the job up. He stared off to the balsam and aspen grove that circled the back yard and rose to the ridge two miles away.

"And Solly?" he asked, still looking at the balsam tips, black, like dagger points against the western sky.

"Can't find 'em," Jack said. "Gone. Went to Chicago some say."

"I'll see how it looks towards the end of the week," Bill finally said. "There's a lot of wood to cut out there. We want 500 taps this year. That's a lot a-boilin'."

Later, at the table she asked how it was going in the woods.

"Hey—you know how I am. A man of the woods, that's what I am. A real livin' Paul Bunyun. Some people can't figure it out—why I like it so much. You have to take charge of things. The first thing I do when steppin' in da woods is give a big yell. Then I yell again when I leave. When my work's done. Hell, yes." With that he looked across the table at her with his frown. The soft light from the kerosene lantern helped accent the shadows on his face. His frown pulled his heavy black eyebrows down over the tops of his eyes. A stare, really.

She rose to get more coffee from the wood-burning range. "We'll be needin' the money," she said, her left palm resting on her distended stomach.

"That kid ain't gonna starve," he retorted as he pointed at her protruding apron with his chin and puckered lips. "There's always something to eat around here."

"He's got only a small batch this time, Bill. Only three or four. They're local horses, not a big truckload of wild ones like last time. No

Dakota horses. It'd be only two or three days. That firewood can wait two or three days."

"Ah, what da hell. Thursday then, damn it. I'll go Thursday. But ten dollars a day. I want more than last time. If he comes out tomorrow you tell him. Ten bucks. These people think I can drop whatever I'm doin', to run and do their dirty work whenever they want. I've got things to do too, dammit. There's always somethin' to do around here but they don't see that. They think Indians just sit around all day. Ten bucks. And if he pushes, you tell him to go to hell. He can kill his own fuckin' horses."

With that he rose and walked to the cupboard where the condensed milk can stood. Soon he was back in his wooden chair by the window at the kitchen table, peering out into the twilight and packing his black pipe. She knew once he started that pipe that the conversation was over. Soon a cloud of sweet-smelling blue smoke rose above him as he sat looking at a newspaper Harry gave him that day. It carried Harry's lunch.

"Okay," she sighed. "I'm goin' up to Ma's for a bit. I'll be back later." She took the lantern from the shelf by the door, found a splinter in the kindling box, opened a range lid to ignite it, then after using it to light the lantern, placed it into the stove and replaced the cast-iron lid. "And, Bill," she said, stepping to the rear door to slip on a brown cloth jacket from a nearby cedar clothes hook on the wall, "what you doin' with that paper? You know you can't read."

The remark caused him to quickly raise his head and look at her as she tied a checkered headscarf at her chin. His eyes sparkled, and a smile creased his face. "Can't what? Get the hell outta here! I can read anything you put in front of me. G'wan—git!" he countered, as the door closed. "Can't read for Christ-sake—I've been reading your mind for years."

THURSDAY MORNING HE was ready when the truck rattled into the yard.

"How many'd you get this time? Five—six?" Bill asked as he slid onto the passenger's seat.

"Only five, Bill. Two broken down teams and a young mare. Oulu horses. Pulp skidders, 'cept for the mare. Got her over the other side of Ashland. Never seen a horse like her. 'Rabian. A real beauty. It's a shame to use her for fox food, but they said they just couldn't break her and finally gave up. I think I'll keep her—try to break 'er m'self."

"Ten bucks a day," Bill abruptly said, giving Jack his heavy-browed stare.

Jack was silent, putting the truck through its gears, as they left the driveway and turned onto the gravel reservation road. "Ten bucks a day?" he asked, pretending surprise.

"That's right. You're taking me away from the sugarbush. There's firewood to cut. Harry can't do it all alone."

Jack considered the demand silently, then knowing there was no one else who would do the hard work, said, "Okay, ten bucks a day."

The sun was still very low when they reached the farm. It was the old Beaulieu place, in the township between the reservation and town. Sumac and aspen were reclaiming its fields and pastures since Jack Sommerfield turned it into a fox farm. Most of the other farmers switched to growing apples, but he took a chance on foxes in the late twenties. There was a good market for fur for all those coats he saw people wearing in the downstate newspapers. So, on certain windy days in fall when the reservation people walked to town for shopping, they alternately caught the sweet smells of ripening Macintoshes and Wealthies along with the sharp, pungent odor of the fox farm.

Jack had to hurry to town to start his shift at the plywood mill, so he quickly showed the horses to Bill. The mare stood in the corral at the side of the barn as Jack pointed out the two large teams. One was a pair of chestnuts, the stallion holding its right front leg up, just resting the tip of the hoof on the ground. The ankle was swollen and festering. The mare had a misshapen right shoulder. An open draining wound that would not heal had formed a small volcano-like ring just behind the shoulder blade.

"Take the chestnuts first," Jack said. "There's plenty of room in the freezer. We'll save the other two for the weekend. That way I can help." Then, more excitedly, he continued, "Look at that little 'Rabian!" as he pointed to a small black horse dwarfed by the huge teams. "Ain't she a beauty?"

Bill saw the smaller black horse standing at the farthest distance in the corral. The morning sunlight glistened off her dark mane as she threw her head up again and again. He saw her warm breath, visible in two streams of steam from her flared nostrils as she breathed steadily in the still cold morning air. Bill thought she resembled pictures he had seen of the fabled Demon's steed, her eyes burning like coals in a small, but hot fire.

"Wild as hell," Jack said. "They got three or four foals out of her but finally gave up. Too much trouble. She just wouldn't settle down. They say no one has ever been able to stay on her, even in all the years they kept her. Mean bitch."

Old Sommerfield paused for a moment or two as he stood with his arms resting on the topmost rung of the corral. Bill noticed the pleasure the old man found in the horse. Then abruptly, Jack said, "Well—I gotta get to town. Be back a little after five to drive you home."

Bill stood at the corral and watched the little mare as the truck rattled from the yard. He was familiar with this work, this old farmyard, with this whole place. He had done this job several times over the past few years, whenever Jack was hard pressed for help. Bill poured himself a cup of coffee from his thermos, then let his gaze move from the corral with its doomed captives to the rows of cages running along the wood-line behind the small barn. There were at least two hundred of them, filled mostly with red and silver foxes and a few brown mink. Earlier he caught the smell as soon as he slid into the truck and now at the farm it was intense. Fox musk. "I should have stood for fifteen," he slowly thought.

"We're goin' more and more to mink," Jack had said in the truck. "The market is better and they don't eat as much. Damn more finicky though. A mink will just lay down and die on you. High strung, and boy, are they ever quick to run. We lost one last week when I forgot to latch the cage. Damn thing was out like a streak, found a hole under the fence and headed for the woods. I can't take many losses like that."

Bill finished the coffee, turned the cup back onto the thermos, then walked to the slaughtering shed to check the tools. It was a weathered, unpainted wooden frame building attached to the west end of the gray, empty barn. The shed had no windows, only a big door facing the yard and a smaller one on the opposite wall toward the weedy cattle yard behind the barn. Brown, dry weeds stood a foot or two above the snow in the yard, where it had not yet been reached by the lengthening day's sun. The shed's floor area was small, only fourteen by twenty-four feet, and a large portion was taken up by an electric meat grinder. The huge, gray cast-iron machine was an investment that Jack Sommerfield felt he had to make to get his fur business going. A walk-in freezer had been installed in the aging barn several years back when Jack purchased the grinder. The two pieces of machinery seemed out of place in the old buildings.

The aged and ailing chestnuts were gentle, and Bill soon had a halter on one and led it to the shed. It was the mare from Oulu, the Finnish settlement out in the flatlands, miles west of the reservation. The cyst on its shoulder was surrounded with black, dried blood and yellow pus, and Bill turned his head away and tried to hold his breath to keep from smelling the offensive odor. The animal, clearly in some pain, let herself be led onto the wooden plank floor next to the grinder and stood docilely while Bill removed the halter, hung it on the wall and then loaded the .22-caliber rifle. The single bullet tore through the brain and the horse dropped immediately. After a few jerky muscle spasms, the big legs stopped churning, and silence filled the small room.

Bill was a worker, and he prided himself in his strength. He brought his pipe and tobacco along to help cut what he knew would be the stench of horse innards, and he took his time carefully lighting up. Once lit, he drew deeply on the pipe while using a small whetstone to put a final edge on a long and narrow-bladed skinning knife. The sound of the stone against fine steel always pleased him. It took him back to earlier days when older people, now long gone, sat in kitchens in evenings and on rainy days, sharpening their tools. Stone on steel—mineral on mineral—he thought, went together. A natural fit.

When the knife was ready he began. First the incisions that circled just above each hoof, then the ring right behind the ears where the neck joined the skull. Then the long incision down the underside of the neck, all the way back to the genitals and finally up around the anal opening. Then it was the incisions down each leg, all the way from the original cut to the hooves. The knife was sharp, but the hide was thick, and it all took time. The horse had turned on its side when falling, and it was easy enough to maneuver around the big legs.

The sharp hooks of a stout block and tackle suspended from a rafter pierced the hide, starting with each hind leg and pulled it off up to the head. The gear-driven lever worked well and with minimal cranking, Bill had the animal skinned, its huge hide lying in a heap beside the carcass. While the body and hide lay steaming, he stood in the doorway to take a breather and reload his pipe. He was sweating now and sought the cool outside air. The yard's birds—the blue jays, chickadees and slate colored juncos—that he had seen before the gunshot, feeding on spilled grain by the granary near the corral, had regained their composure and were eating once again. Bill glanced up at the sky for signs of crows and ravens that would surely discover the butchering going on today, and would come to inspect anything tossed back into the cow yard. For some reason he liked these black birds, especially the ravens. They often stood by when he was in the woods, perched in the tree heights, watching him like curious sentinels.

Bill leaned against the doorframe and surveyed the yard as he drew upon his pipe. Half and Half. Half tobacco and half horseshit, he liked to say. He watched smoke lazily curl up from the pipe's bowl just as smoke lazily curled up from the chimney of the faded white clapboard house that stood at the front of the farmyard. The column rose about seventy-five feet before flattening out to form a gray cloud above the house. He looked for activity at the kitchen windows and backdoor but caught no movement.

150

After another cup of the thermos's coffee, he returned to his job, but not until he slipped into a pair of tall rubber boots and a long rubber apron. When he made the abdominal incision the black blood, gushing like a new spring freshet, spilled onto the planked floor. Bill worked quickly now, alternately holding his breath and drawing on the pipe. He forgot about the offensive fox smell as the mare's body released its life's odors. "Damn," he said to himself as he turned his head away again and again.

He was sweating harder now, and was bloodied, and the room filled with even more heat and steam. The mare was opened, and its organs oozed out onto the floor, joining the blood. As he turned to the rear of the horse to sever the last few tissues holding the mass of innards he saw her through the steam, standing in the doorway. She was a black silhouette against the day's light. He turned back to the carcass and began to disjoint the limbs. Conscious of her presence, he kept his back to the door while he bent to his work.

"Stopping for lunch, aren't you?" she finally asked. "Not going to work through your lunch hour, are you?"

Rising, he slowly turned to face her in the doorway, the knife in his bloodied hand. "Ya, okay," he said, as their eyes briefly met. Sweat ran down his face, making streaks in the splattered blood. In spite of Harry's warning, he saw again that she was beautiful. *Why?* he wondered. Jack was such a rough, tobacco-chewing man, dirty and usually smelly. What kept her?

He placed the knife on the shelf along the shed's wall and stepped outside to remove the heavy apron and boots. Once the apron was off and hanging on an outside nail, he sat on a rough wooden bench beside the shed to pull off the messy boots. He slipped on his leather work shoes, not bothering to tie them. Rarely wearing gloves except in the coldest weather, his hands, wrists and forearms were bloodied up to his sleeves that were rolled at his elbows.

"I have some warm water in the house, William. You can wash up."

Still sitting on the bench he raised his eyes to the old fields beyond the yard. William! *For Chris'sake*, he thought, only his mother and the nuns ever called him that.

"Did you bring a lunch?" she continued.

"Ya, I'm fine. I'll just wash up a little here by the pump," he replied, pointing with his chin to the rusty hand pump standing in the center of the yard. "I got enough to eat."

"Well, I made a big kettle of vegetable soup, knowing you were coming. Are you sure?" she said.

"No, no. That's all right. I'm okay."

"Jack always wants us to feed our help. He'd be mad if I didn't give you lunch. Come on in; it's ready."

"No, no," he repeated, rising to walk to the pump.

"I'll bring you a bowl to eat with your sandwiches," she insisted as she walked back to the house.

Bill did not protest, seeing it was hopeless. As he bent at the pump to clean his hands and arms, he thought about what Harry had said the day before. "White meat," he had kidded. "Solly was on the trail of white meat."

Taking his time at the pump, he carefully removed the blood, then used the dented aluminum dipper hung on a bent wire affixed to the body of the pump to refresh himself with its icy water. He drank a dipperful, then bent for another as he used his right arm to work the pump handle and his left to catch the rushing water.

Walking back to the bench at the shed, he saw her come out of the house's back door and move carefully down the porch's few wooden steps. She held a large ceramic bowl of soup, steaming, before her. He knew the soup would taste good. At the bench, he opened his brown sack lunch to arrange the bacon-grease sandwiches and small glass container of his wife's homemade sweet pickles. As he reached to accept the bowl of hot soup, he held it on his knees for a second as she went to a pocket at her breast for the silver spoon she brought for him.

"There," she said, approvingly, looking at the soup, then to him.

"Wah," he exclaimed, appreciatively. "It's big enough. *Megwetch*."

She had been in the area long enough to learn a few of the Ojibwe words the reservation people sometimes shared with Whites. His sincere thanks were accepted with a nod of her head.

"Well, I'll let you eat," she said almost sadly, he thought. Then she suddenly turned and walked quickly to the house.

Bill relaxed with the welcomed food. It made an excellent complement to the dry sandwiches, and the warmth of the noon sunshine made a nice contrast to the cool March breezes that now and then moved about the yard. Then, after the food and another pipe of tobacco, he slowly put his boots and apron back on.

The electric grinder accepted the smaller pieces of flesh from the dismembered horse with ease. Bill used an ax to cut through the heavy limb bones and the machine took them, too. Sommerfield said the finely ground bones provided needed minerals to the foxes and mink. Even though the grinder was a large, heavy one, meant for this sort of work, it took over an hour to reduce the huge cadaver to pieces small enough to feed into it and for the machine to complete its task. Its stainless steel hopper had to be emptied a few times, the red and white mash of meat and bones dumped into a metal cart with wheels. From this cart the ground meat was shoveled into heavy metal tubs that were stored in the freezer.

Finally, Bill removed most of the waste from the intestine, and forked the slippery mass, along with the stomach, lungs and heart into the machine. At last it was finished. The horse was gone, transformed into ground meat. Even the hooves and head—once he had removed most of its hide—were put through the machine. The big grinder was hot and needed a well-earned rest, needed to cool.

It was almost four o'clock when he began to wash down the killing room floor. The cold water, carried in buckets from the pump, then splashed onto the floor, washed the blood and smaller bits of residue through the back door, into the weedy barnyard. The grinder was washed as well, prepared for tomorrow's work.

It took some effort to drag the heavy hide into the farmyard to be stretched out beside the barn to dry. This would be rolled, tied and eventually sold to a leather worker in Ashland.

Bill was puzzled about the head and hooves. Jack had said to grind them. Other times he wanted them hauled to the rear of the farm to be dumped into a swampy low spot that, for years, was the farm's dumping ground. It was not a completely unpleasant job for Bill, since he knew this refuse would be the food for the winged and four-legged ones. The ravens and crows, as well as the smaller birds—even the little chickadees—fed upon it, and he once found tracks of wild fur bearers at the dump as well. He wondered if the few timber wolves still in the area came to feed.

But this time Jack told him to grind up all the horse, even the head and hooves. He didn't say why, but Bill thought it would be related to money. The foxes and mink would eat it all, and the grinder could handle it. So this time the birds and animals of the woods would have to look elsewhere for their meal. Old Sommerfield did not think much of them and their needs.

When working with the hide beside the barn, Bill noticed her standing by the house, on the southern side, where the early spring sun's warmth melted the snow. This is where her flower garden was. Now she was moving over it, stooping to poke here and there in the brown leaves and dead grass from last season's growth, searching for signs of another year's shoots. She spent much time on her flowers. Bill knew the yard was filled with them from spring to fall.

When she stood to move to the wooden grape arbor at the garden's edge, her black hair glistened in the late afternoon sunlight, and her fair complexion was visible like a single whitecap on a shadowed sea. *How old is this woman?* he mused. Her slenderness told of much life still ahead—a new shoot with the glory of the entire summer before it. Then, after coming back to the shed, as he stopped to tamp one more pipefull of tobacco, Bill wondered if old Sommerfield took his tobacco chew out before going to bed.

154

Now free from the heavy boots and apron, Bill once more washed his hands, arms, and face at the pump, before coming back to the bench. He sat in the comfortable sunlight, the welcome feeling of a good day's work completed, while he gently renewed the skinning knife's edge with the whetstone. After carefully spitting onto the small flat, soft gray stone as he held it in his left palm, he placed the knife blade onto the stone and started the slow circular motion with his right hand. The knife slowly took on its sharpness again, ready for tomorrow.

Finishing with the knife, he checked the edges of the ax and other hand tools he had used throughout the day. Finally completed, he walked out to the corral to rest as he leaned on the top rail, looking at the three remaining horses. There was still a half-hour or so before Sommerfield returned from the mill.

"You staying for supper?" her voice asked at his side, her arm brushing his as it rested on the top rail. He had seen her coming from the house but thought better of turning to greet her. He stood, leaning on the rail, his back to the house, waiting for her arrival.

"Oh—ah—I'm . . ." he stammered.

"If you don't mind soup again—"

"No, I'm expected," he finally said.

They did not look at each other as they spoke. Their eyes were on the Arabian keeping her distance at the far side of the corral. She was nervously pawing the ground again.

"I'd better get started on the feeding. Would you care to help?" she asked, turning to peer into his eyes.

"Ya, sure," Bill replied, looking directly back to her. This time they held the strong eye contact for a moment past what would have been needed; would have been normal. Then she turned and walked to the barn.

He found the small, wheeled wooden wagon used for feeding the foxes and pulled it to the freezer. She was already there with a tub of meat, still emitting little rising wisps of steam as it cooled. They loaded two more tubs before he pulled the wagon to the yard's pump. A thirty-five-gallon, open-top metal drum sat beside the old pump. He loaded it onto the cart beneath the pump's spout and began to work the pump's handle. After filling the barrel he slowly pulled the now heavy cart along the path back to the cages behind the barn. She had gone ahead to wait for him, holding the gate open.

"I'm finally getting used to the smell," she said, as she began to scoop a portion of the flesh out for each caged fox. She rapped the ladle onto the cage tops, letting the meat fall through the wire to flat metal plates, secured to the cages' floors. Bill used a bucket to dip out the water from the barrel and began to fill the cups that each cage held.

"How long's it been now?" he asked. "Two, three years?" as he continued with the watering.

"Two and a half in June," she replied, as she too, kept at the feeding chore.

He pulled the cart to the next row of cages, the woman walking behind. Most of the foxes came to the front of the cage and began to eat the food. Some stayed curled in their wooden sleeping compartments at the rear, their pointed noses sticking out from the round openings.

Bill had helped with the feeding before, and it always saddened him to be this close to the caged foxes. They lived on meshed wire. Wire worlds for padded feet that usually walked on the forest floor. Fox eyes peered at him from the dark interiors of the sleeping boxes. Some boxes appeared to be empty, but they were there, he knew, watching him. Unlike him, she seemed not to be troubled. Perhaps she understood better than he, but he could not be so aloof. *Wagoosh*, they were called in Ojibwe. *Wagoosh*, is the old word for the fox.

"Bill," she shouted from the end of the row, "come here."

He set the watering bucket down and walked to her.

"The new mink," she said, as he came up to stand beside her. "Silver. This is the male. That's the female," she continued, pointing to the next cage.

This was the first time he saw the mink. Much smaller than the foxes, more sleek and pristine looking, they hesitated to come out of

156

their dark boxes, but once teased into the daylight they paced the cages like lions in zoos.

"I've never seen a silver mink before," Bill quietly said. "Fur coats for high society." They stood together admiring the sleek animals.

Finally she broke the silence with, "Breeding stock. They're breeding stock. He won't kill them." She slowly put her hand on his arm, then, seemingly enthralled by the animals' beauty, went on. "Jack got them from New Jersey. He thinks a lot of these two mink."

They were almost finished when the pickup rattled into the yard. Old Somerfield drove Bill home and said he'd be by early in the morning to pick him up.

The next day, Friday, Bill slaughtered the chestnut stallion. It was a warmer day and the work was harder. He took more breathers, standing or sitting by the killing shed's door, smoking and sipping coffee. Then, just before lunch, the grinder broke down. He was feeding a portion of a large hindquarter into it, when it simply stopped turning. The electric motor kept humming, so he knew it was a gear or pin of some sort. The machine's breakdown's were not unknown, for Solly had a few stories about these delays. A year ago, Bill himself, repaired it. Solly often complained of such mishaps.

He thought he should tell the woman, so he walked to the house and knocked at the kitchen door. He heard a quick, "Come in," but hesitated, and knocked again. She came to the door and, after hearing the story, said the wrenches were somewhere in the machine shed.

Soon after he carried the wooden box of hand tools to the killing shed and started trouble-shooting, she appeared, ready to help. They worked together, she sometimes wrestling with a heavy box wrench trying to loosen a large nut, or else carefully replacing an oily gasket and bolting a shaft cover back into place.

"I didn't know you were a mechanic," he said as he lay on his back on the oak planking underneath the grinder.

"There's a lot you don't know about me," she responded. She was on her knees beside him, holding a flashlight, directing its beam into the darkness where Bill was struggling to open a gear-box housing. This was the last hope, for they had checked everything else and found no problems. It took the better part of an hour, and his hands, like hers, were marked with the machine's black grease.

The hour of repair work, however, went well. As one or the other climbed over and under the machine, handing a wrench or holding a light, sometimes grunting in an effort to loosen a fitting, they started to anticipate each other's moves, started to jell as a team.

Suddenly Bill exclaimed, "Here it is! It's this damn pin—look," he said as he wriggled out, holding up a broken rectangular, one-half inch shear pin. "Do you have one of these around here somewhere?" he asked, placing the two pieces of the pin in her outstretched hand.

"Finally," she said, eagerly sharing his pleasure with the discovery. "There are all kinds of boxes of bolts and things in the machine shed. Let's have a look."

They quickly walked past the corral to the machine shed and started going through small wooden boxes holding nails, bolts, screws, washers, and numerous steel parts from unknown tools and machines. In time they found one of brass cotter keys and steel rectangular shear pins. Then, there it was, just the size needed.

"Yup, this'll do," he said, holding both the broken and sound pin up to the sky to get a better look. "Same size. We got lucky."

"Let me see," she said, extending a dirty hand to him. She took the hard steel pins and examined them as he had, as if she were a skilled machinist. They hurried back to the killing shed and in little time had the pin installed and the machine working.

Bill could see that she was loose now and completely at ease. The hour or so of labor had done it: the working together under honest doubt and strain, followed by the joy of completion. After switching the machine on again and assuring that it was working properly, Bill stood back with her for a moment to simply enjoy it. Then he said, "Hard steel pins. D'ja ever think about them—'bout what they do?" He brought his eyebrows down over his eyes like he did when he was relaxed and freely contemplating something he enjoyed. "Their whole purpose," he went on, "is to lock gear and shaft together and hold them tight as if they were one. But, if the strain is too much they must snap. They break—Pow!—right in two. They save money. They must break so the more expensive parts don't."

"Sometimes I think machines are built better than people," she added.

By now it was well past noon, and after using some gasoline and rags to clean their greasy hands, she insisted he join her for the last of the soup. Bill hesitated and once again said he would eat his sandwiches outside on the bench, but that he would take some of that soup. She went to the house and momentarily appeared with two large bowls, came to the bench and sat down beside him, ignoring his uneasiness.

"God damn that Solly!" he said to himself. "His takin' off for Chicago got me into this." But by now, Bill's defenses were down. He saw no harm in eating lunch with this woman, outside on a warm March day, only a few weeks away from spring.

Maybe Bill never really believed Harry's stories about Solly and her, about Solly's supposed quest for white meat. *Harry said she was hungry, would get after poor Solly now and then, but look at this woman!* Bill thought. *She's almost Indian. She's different. She's not uppity. She could be one of us.*

After eating lunch and walking to the pump for a drink of good, cold water, Bill said he'd better get back to work. Most of the grinding was yet to be done. He told her he thought the pin broke because he overloaded the machine, especially with a big piece of one of the leg bones, so he would have to go slower and be more careful.

She took the bowls to the house and to his surprise soon appeared back at the shed dressed in an old shirt, denim work pants and rubber boots, intending to work with him. He said nothing, letting her have her way, but he began to think about what Old Summerfield would say with her out here like this. It was true what Harry said about his not leaving her off the place unless he was along. Bill hoped they would finish the work so she would be back in the house before Jack came home.

By working steadily, although more slowly, they finished the heavy work just before four o'clock. Bill started to relax a bit as they both walked to the pump to clean up, but then the pickup truck unexpectedly appeared down the dirt road and turned into the yard.

The woman was noticeably concerned, and when her hands and arms were cleaned she hurriedly walked to the barn to start the afternoon feeding. Bill was walking back to the shed to drag out the hide and wash the floor and machine when Sommerfield fell in step with him. It was immediately apparent that the old man had spent some time in one of the town's taverns instead of putting in a full shift at the mill.

"What's goin' on?" Sommerfield asked. "What was she doin' out here?"

"The damn grinder broke down. I asked her to help finish up, get the work done before it got too late," Bill lied. "The shear pin on that big gear way underneath snapped. We found one in the shed." With that Jack left Bill and hurried over to the barn where she was loading the cart. Soon Bill could hear his loud shouting, but he did not hear her offer any reply.

Sommerfield had the truck running as Bill finished cleaning up. On the ride home, nothing was said about the woman. Bill tried to be quiet, to let the old man go on and on about those damn fools running the mill, about how they knocked off early some days when work was slow.

"A man can't hardly get his forty hours in some weeks with that," complained Jack. "Those big shots jerk us around like we were nothin'." Then he told Bill, "Let's leave the other team 'til next week. There's enough in the freezer for now. Maybe next week, I'll get you for the others."

"When will I get paid?" Bill asked.

"I'll have it tomorrow," Sommerfield said. "I'll bring it out tomorrow morning early, before nine."

The next day Bill waited most of the morning, then decided to walk the three miles to the fox farm for his pay. Most of the reserve's people had no cars or trucks, so they usually walked to town on Saturday to do some shopping and just to get out for a while. He and his wife fell into step with a few others as they started out on what was a beautiful spring day. Bill would turn off at the fox farm road and make the loop into town to catch them on the way back.

He liked to stretch his legs on these walks, liked to be out in the air, to be with his wife and friends. There was always talk and laughter on these trips. He made the fox farm turn-off and soon was in the Sommerfield yard, climbing the back steps and knocking at the kitchen door. After some delay it opened only a crack.

She was surprised to see him, and when he mentioned the pay, she went to get it. In a moment or so, she was back with twenty dollars in cash, and as she opened the door further to hand it out he saw the bruises. One eye was swollen, turning blue and awful looking, a cut on her puffed lower lip. He tipped his head a bit and saw she was sobbing, both eyes red and teary. She tried to keep Bill from noticing.

"Damn!" he said loudly in surprise. "What did he do to you? Where is that old bastard?"

"Shhh—" she quickly uttered. "No-no—he's sleeping it off. After taking you home he went back into town and came home late. He had too much."

Bill didn't move.

"Go home, William," she continued, "I'll be all right. I'm okay."

With that she closed the door. He stood momentarily still. After raising his closed hand to knock again, he paused, then turned to move down the steps. "That damn fool," Bill said out loud. "Harry was right. He is nuts!"

Walking to the corral he paused briefly to study the little Arabian mare, to admire its lines, its spirit. The horse was much too fine for Old Sommerfield, he thought, much to fine. Then as his anger grew even more, he quickly walked out to the fox cages, found the new breeding pair of mink, and without any hesitation opened both their doors. It took only moments for them to notice, and they were out, onto the ground, running along the fence to the gate he had left open. He watched their sleek, silver bodies gently bobbing as they sped over the last of the late winter's snow. Soon they were only dark specks on the white. Then they were at the distant woodline and gone.

๛ 18 ๙

The Last of the Free Ones

Freedom was just a natural part of life,
without anything un-free as a comparison.

—Wub-e-ke-niew, 1995

 a comin'?" he asked, looking me straight in the eyes.

"Sure," I answered quickly, realizing the question was his assent to my going.

We were on our hands and knees beneath the ancient Whitney Crab tree that stands beside my mother-in-law's small wood-framed house on the Red Cliff Reservation. This was far northern Wisconsin, and cold Lake Superior was only 200 yards away. The lawn had not been cut recently so we searched for the gnarled and wormy apples.

"Ya got a gun?" he asked, standing up, this time relieving me of his stare as he tilted his head to see which branch to shake next.

"There's one in the house," I answered, "a twelve gauge with slugs." That satisfied him.

We poured the apples from the cardboard box into sacks he pulled from his faded Oldsmobile. The car, like him, was of an early vintage, large and imposing, with numerous dents and spots. The wheel covers were gone, the upholstery torn and stained, and the trunk littered with ends of rope, yellow plastic oil cans, and the finer bits of bark from firewood. The car had an antiquated bigness, a dignity of the past. We filled two burlap sacks and one large red-mesh onion bag with the bumpy apples and after they were tied, laid them to rest in the trunk beside the bald spare tire.

"Let me get the gun," I said as I hurried to the house.

"Bring a light," he shouted after me.

On the way out, I grabbed a jacket from the back shed, and soon we were rumbling along the blacktop heading north out of the village.

I WAS WITH WEEB MARTIN, a seventy-one-year-old Ojibwe man married to a first cousin of my wife. So we were kin, and in some unclear way it was a relationship that seemed to work. I had known Weeb for over thirty years. He was a solid, sensitive man who was, at times, loud, brash and downright vulgar. He used any kind of language in front of just about anyone. His presence was felt in the community though he never held a seat on the tribal council or any other sort of official position.

As he directed the Oldsmobile along the forest-lined roadway, I was reminded how the years had changed him. The black hair had turned gray, and, although his face, with its prominent nose was still strong, it was noticeably wrinkled and suggested a quietness that came with a lived life. I saw that he, too, as with most things, had withered with time. Like the apple trees, his was an untended appearance—not dirty or messy, just untended.

Weeb, I thought, who sired several children and watched them grow, had never worked an eight-to-five job, had never punched a time clock, had never worn a union button. Still, he had worked hard. I recalled when, several years before when we were peeling pulp, I had become exhausted on the second day. He laughed at me. "What the hell ya doin' in the woods? You're a city dweller," he chided. "Ya better go back before we have to carry ya outta here."

Two miles out of the village, he pulled into his driveway and turned off the engine. "I'll be right out," he said as he left the car and hurried to his small house. The single-story, wood-frame structure was sided with dark-green roofing paper. In places the glassy granules had worn away, exposing the blackness beneath. Goldenrod, in full bloom, quietly nestled beside the house's foundation as if planted there, like the pampered petunias and marigolds in town. It was late August, the week before Labor Day weekend, and it had been a warm day, but already the evening told of a cool night. Weeb soon returned with a seasoned deer rifle, a large orange, plastic flashlight and an old, patched denim jacket.

"Since I been settin' out apples, I see their sign each morning. They come in at night. We should get some," he said.

He had been cutting firewood in the tribal woodlot all week, and it was time to start laying in his winter's supply of venison—something he did with ease. Deer meat. I'd eaten many meals at his wife's table, and over the years she'd rarely served beef—lots of venison and, of course, the Indian favorite, pork. To some reservation dwellers, beef was "*Chimokemaan* meat"—white man's meat.

It took about twenty minutes of slow driving to get to the wood-lot. Just north of the Martin house, the road narrowed and turned to gravel. He finally pulled to the side and stopped by a trail that led toward the lake. "We could drive in, but they'd smell this thing. Too much of their brother's blood spilled in the trunk," he said.

We carried our guns, lights, jackets, and the apples about an eighth of a mile into the woods. A good-sized pile of eight-foot white- and yellow-birch poles, mixed with young, manageable red-oak logs was stacked by the trail. The appealing aroma of fresh-cut wood hung in the heavy evening air, and small light-colored mounds of sawdust, the kind with large chips made by a sharp chainsaw blade, littered the ground around numerous new stumps. Smaller piles lay in a line moving away from each stump, showing the length of the log that had been measured and cut.

"Ahhh, these apples are nice and ripe. They should bring 'em in. Dump a bag by that stump and another over by the trail by the old pile."

I did as he directed while he carried the third sack to a cluster of birch stumps about twenty-five feet away. Soon we had three piles of aromatic red apples in a rough circle in the middle of the clearing. It was getting dark, and I knew the afterglow would leave us in an hour or so. Luckily, there would be a moon.

"You'll have to build a platform," he said, puckering his lips in the Ojibwe way, as he pointed with his chin to an oak standing at the north edge of the clearing. "Where's your hammer and nails?" he kidded, looking surprised.

Weeb liked to remind me of who I was. "A *Chimoke* can't build anything without a hammer and nails," he laughed, as he walked to the stacked wood and quickly pulled out a small single-bit cruising ax before reaching into a side pocket for a sharp, folded knife. Before long, he assembled a little platform made of small, straight birch poles, lashed together with strips cut and torn from one of the burlap sacks. I stood in amazement as he quickly assembled what, for me, was a beautiful bit of woodcraft. He helped wedge it into the lower branches of the oak tree about nine feet off the ground.

"Get up there," he ordered. "See if you have a clear view."

I scrambled up, helped by a boost, and after using the ax to remove a few smaller branches, I had a commanding view of all three piles. He handed up my shotgun and light.

"How about my jacket?" I asked, pointing to where it lay on the firewood pile.

"Jacket? Hey, it's summer. What the hell you want a jacket for?" he laughed as he stepped to retrieve it.

"Weeb," I said, "I remember the last time I was out with you— I froze my ass."

He chuckled disparagingly as he tossed up my coat. I watched him walk to the woodpile to pick up his gun, light, and jacket. "Just remember where I am," he shouted as he pointed to his tree with his gun. "If you shoot, shoot down, not up, and for Christ sake, not over here," he continued, as he used his rifle to point up to his platform.

166

Soon we were both sitting in our trees, backs against the trunks, knees under our chins. The small, round birch poles told me I was resting on hard wood, and before long I folded my jacket and used it as a cushion. I could see him, about seventy-five to 100 feet away, sitting still, his jacket, flashlight, and rifle at his feet. He looked relaxed and completely at ease. I wondered about how many times he had done this sort of thing, staked out somewhere in the Red Cliff woods, listening to the night, waiting to kill deer. Who taught him how to select the spot and to be still for hours on end in the darkness?

He was born on the reservation in 1918. His family was among the most traditional ones, but not traditional in the tourist sense. Weeb was not like some who danced at the new powwows. I never saw him or any of his immediate family dance. Instead, he was traditional in a subsistence-like, woods-way. Like the deer, he knew how to survive in the woods, and his traditionalism was not a consciously planned thing. He was simply doing what he had been taught. He was using the land and animals around him in order to survive. As I saw his darkening form perched in his tree, I knew I was witnessing something passing, as surely as his outdated automobile.

Weeb had been raised early in the twentieth century far before the Indian renaissance of the 1970s. He was a young lad in the times of Christian teaching, times of stern priests and strict nuns. He could not cast all that aside—to do so would have been to deny his parents and other elders long gone. So, he was not like some of the young new reservation folks who turned their backs on the church, who preferred to wear their hair in long braids and who conspicuously wore beadwork and carried new gebic bags.

The sun's afterglow had completely gone, yet I could still make out the shadowy forms of the clearing's stumps with their apple piles. The nearly full moon in the east peeked between clouds that soared across the night sky. Then I heard a sudden rustling below. An *ajidamoo*, a red squirrel, had come to investigate the fresh apples. He scurried here and there, inspecting each pile. Then, after several minutes of loud scolding, settled down to eat his fill.

Later, it must have been near midnight, I heard an owl. It was very close—"Ko-ko' ko-ooo', ko-ko' ko-kooo'," it said. A scary call, yet appealing. I thought of an incident from several years past, how a brother-in-law attempted to calm a restless child by telling him an owl was outside in the tree. "Sssh," he hushed the crying youngster, "the owl's out there." Some held the belief that the owl brought death, but owl stories conflicted as I recalled a Dakota friend who insisted the owl was a good sign. He said that when one called, especially in the west, it was a time of honesty—of truth. "When an owl calls," he claimed, "you can't lie. You might try, but only truth will come out."

In certain Ojibwe origin teachings the owl brought knowledge of medicinal plants to the people. This was essential to this woodland culture, for plants were used to heal, and the owl, in a wonderful paradox, brought both life and death.

Suddenly, just above me came a loud *whoosh*, strong feathers outstretched to catch the wind. *He's flown to my tree!* I thought. *He's right here!* Immediately after the rush of wind, I heard the soft thud of his feet as they grasped a branch—it seemed only a yard or two above. "Ko-ko'—ko-ooo'," he called again, this time so loud I thrilled with an ecstatic coldness that prickled my skin. "Ko-ko'—ko-ooo'," his call resounded, loud and deep, again and again. "Damn," I said to myself, daring not to move. Soon I heard a call from the direction of Weeb's tree—"Ko-ko'-ko-ooo'—ko-ko'—ko-ooo'." It had to be Weeb, playing with this owl, but my owl was not responding. With another sudden rush, he was up, out of my tree and gone. Shocked by what had just happened, I wanted to laugh and yell at Weeb, but I kept silent. It would be something to talk about later.

No other sounds came from Weeb's direction. He was quiet over there in the dark. This contrasted sharply with a time several years before when he celebrated his sixtieth birthday. His wife grew tired of his roughness and threw him out. He had been drinking wine for days—it was right after pulp-cutting season when he had some cash—and I found him at Jenkins', the general store and bar just outside the southern boundary of the reserve. I heard his laugh even before I got to the porch steps.

Upon entering the little store, I saw him seated with two other older men, on wooden ginger ale cases, set on their ends as seats, in a half circle beside the shelves of canned goods and cereal boxes that lined three of the store's short walls. His friends could do little but laugh and listen as he loudly went on and on about one thing after another—cursing at will—using the sort of language that was his trademark.

Later that afternoon when the wine began to take its toll and when his friends left him, he stumbled into my mother-in-law's yard and sat at the weathered picnic table under the apple tree. He was silent, just sitting there, staring at the lake. After a while I went out to greet him and take him a cup of coffee. Without speaking, he shifted his piercing gaze from the water to me, took the cup and kept staring. I was familiar with his stare and could usually handle it, but that time I failed. His face was flushed, and his heavy, gray, canopy-like eyebrows shaded his eyes. He reminded me of an aged eagle, his large, beaked nose commanding some response from his prey—and I had to look away.

Then, steadily, he rose to lean across the table, and before I could react, he reached over, quickly grabbed my head with both of his big hands and placed a hard kiss on the side of my face. No words were uttered. He sat down and finally released me from his stare as he sipped the hot coffee. That was Weeb Martin, so loud at times that he drove people away, yet at others times he could be so silent that his presence was a plunging knife that laid bare one's soul.

My THOUGHTS WENT BACK TO THE NIGHT. A slow breeze moved the treetops as I strained to see movement below. Nothing. No deer. Weeb recently took one of his sons on such a trip as this but became upset when the young man lit a cigarette. "The damn fool," he said as he told the story later, "he needed a smoke so bad!"

Once when I asked Weeb why he did not smoke, he laughed, then said, "I can't afford to both drink and smoke. I'm a poor man." I had never seen him use tobacco as an offering in the woods or on the lake. He was the sort of man who could understand a tobacco offering and not belittle it, yet I felt he would never make one himself. He was a Christian—a Catholic, and Catholics did not usually make offerings of tobacco. I knew that such offerings were becoming more common again on the reservation when people hunted, fished and even took trees and other plants from the woods. Was Weeb more "real" than they? I pondered this, concluding that somehow this man, this aged, invisible Ojibwe man perched in an oak tree in the darkness was more honest, more traditional than some of the younger ones who had left the church to drum and have their own ceremonies.

Where were they tonight? I thought, as my mind saw these new-traditionals at the tribal casino and large, comfortable liquor lounge. *How often had they sat shivering underneath an owl in the dark woods?* Some of them occasionally hunted and were eating venison again, but Weeb had always eaten it. Some of the villagers did not prefer it, feeling, I'm certain, that it was Indianish—a derogatory word pronounced "Indi-on-ish"— meaning it was old-fashioned and backward to like deer meat. Venison, especially if from an older animal, had a certain wild taste that was offensive to some. These modern Indians respected deer meat—it was about the sanctity of ancestors and traditions, yet many really preferred beef. They would eat venison quietly on holidays with wild rice and the favored lake trout, whitefish, and fried bread. But I had always known Weeb to prefer venison. Did he do it out of some sort of resentment? Was it another indication of his steadfastness, like his stare, his desire not to change, to be honest and true to how he had been taught to live?

Soon I grew tired of this musing. All I knew was that I was very sleepy, stiff, and downright cold. I put the jacket on, making a bit of noise as I shifted my weight to my knees. My rump was again submitted to the hardness of the birch poles, but I was glad for the warmth of the coat as I felt my flashlight and gun at my feet before I stuffed my hands into my pockets.

I could still make out the mounds of apples in the darkness. The red squirrel, long since filled with the fruit, was gone, probably bedded down for the night. *Where the hell are the deer?* I asked myself. Had Wenebozho, the trickster, warned them to stay away? I closed my eyes and rested my chin on my chest. I wondered about falling asleep and slipping off the platform, crashing to the ground. It's not impossible, I concluded, but luckily, the platform was large enough, so I curled into the fetal position and laid on my side.

H<small>EY, WAKE UP! HOW YA GOIN'</small> ta' see the deer when you're asleep?" It was Weeb shouting from his tree—his beam of light pouring onto me like a large floodlight in the darkness. "Let's get the hell outta here," he continued as I saw him start to climb down.

"They must a gone south tonight. I guess they don't like our wormy apples," he said as he waited for me to climb down. "Those farmers must get all the deer they want," he went on, referring to the white fruit growers who operated apple orchards just south of the reserve, towards town.

We stood for a few moments to relieve our bladders and enjoy the bright stars. It was well past midnight, and I was eager to get home. I fell in behind Weeb as we started out on the trail back to the car.

There was no complaint about the truant deer, only acceptance of our empty-handedness. We were silent as we slowly walked along. I breathed deeply of the heavy, pungent forest odors, enjoying their rich moistness at this special time when the night would soon be ready to give way to day. The talk and laughter about the owl would have to wait for the ride home.

19

Island Views

We are not part of a play. We stand here
in front of you.

—Tom Peacock, 2002

T WAS JUST TOO HOT in the gym, too hot for a crowd that big. "God," Dosh Ojibbeway said to himself, "all this body heat," but he toughed it out, staying for the chance to see the old photos, the pictures of how the rez was back then. Reggie LaRiche said they were really good, that one even showed Great Uncle Zim in his World War I uniform. Uncle Zim LaRiche never came back from France, being buried somewhere over there.

Reggie saw the pictures under the big tent outside Washburn last week at the show's premier viewing. In the last few years, he developed an eye for old photos. He said he became interested down at Eau Claire in some of his classes. He started to pay attention in a history class when the professor came in with a carousel full of slides made from black-and-white photographs he found in Madison buried in the historical society. Now, years later, Reggie was still at it, tracking down old rez photos, copying them, even writing a little about them. He was trying to make sense of it all.

Dosh took a seat near the back door, up in the side bleachers with the rest of the small contingent of rez people. The gym floor was nearly half filled with folding chairs, and the white townspeople were using them. Most of the locals, even the orchard growers from out in the country, had seen the show the week before over in Washburn. Reggie was included in that first showing because he called himself a journalist since he started the monthly newsletter for the tribe.

It was a musical show, the sort popular these days. It had a simple script, read by a cast of four readers, and was backed up by a small folksy musical ensemble made up mostly of strings and woodwinds with a concertina and a little brass thrown in. While the music and reading were going on either on stage or, as in the case that day, right on the gym floor in front of the tiny orchestra, the photos were projected onto a large screen that stood behind the musicians.

It was meant to be upbeat, celebrating the land and the people that came here. So far Reggie had withheld judgment on it, waiting perhaps, for the dust to settle a bit before he shared his real thoughts. But he said it was clear that the townspeople loved it. After the older black-and-white photos ended and the more recent colored ones started to appear, they laughed approvingly with the recognition of familiar faces, photos of friends and relatives.

Finally, a little after one o'clock, the gym lights were turned off and the music began. Then suddenly came the first pictures, large colorful views of the big lake and its islands. Taken from the air, they showed the rich blues and greens that had become hallmarks for the tourist industry promotions. Soon the black-and-whites started to appear as a voice began telling about the coming of the French. Dosh was treated to quick views of the series of the early explorers, sketches mostly, of what they might have looked like: Brule and Duluth; Radisson and Groseilliers. Father Claude Allouez was shown, and the martyr, Father Rene Menard, who disappeared somewhere inland in northern

Wisconsin back in 1660. After a few others, like Schoolcraft and Baraga, the over-used photo of Chief Buffalo suddenly appeared, the one with the crack running through his lower face, the torn paper making it look like he was grimacing with pain.

Well, Dosh thought, *Buffalo still looks the same after all these years. They sure like that old photo.*

Then came a few lively musical numbers supporting the familiar pictures of the logging sleds with their huge loads of gigantic, white pine logs piled high. The usual photos of the numerous sawmills were sprinkled in, and a humorous shot or two of cows on the town's main street in the 1800s. Blonde-haired Swedes and darker Europeans standing outside their shops were part of the photos that started to show the audience a few of the main-street buildings still standing in town.

Then suddenly the crowd was shown the Island View Hotel on a hillside overlooking the big lake. Apparently its size was especially noteworthy because it was given not only a goodly portion of the narrated script, but it even had its own song that sung its praises and told of the national celebrities who came to take lodging in its fancy, spacious rooms. The Island View was kept on the screen longer than most of the other photos, and Dosh leaned forward to peer at it. Reggie said to watch for it. His family knew the photo, had been told of the old hotel with its four tiers of outside balconies facing the lake. When in her late teens, Grandma LaRiche worked as a domestic—a chambermaid—in the big building. Although she was gone, her stories of the days of the Island View were kept alive in the family.

Dosh squinted to see better the white-bloused women up on one of the balconies. Was it Grandma LaRiche, standing there with a few of her friends, taking a breather from cleaning the rooms? Did she and her rez friends meet Mrs. Lincoln and General Sherman? Did they make their beds? Dump their chamberpots?

Then came the photos from World War I, and to Dosh's frustration, the black-and-white of Uncle Zim. Just for an instant he stood, thin, unsmiling in his wool uniform, his lower legs wrapped in the style of the soldiers back then. Even in black and white, Dosh saw the uniform's olive-drab color, but it was only an instant. Uncle Zim had been given his cameo appearance. In a flash he was gone.

Dosh was soon treated to photos of life in town in the 1920s, the 1930s, and into World War II. Now the gym audience was into the show, despite the uncomfortable heat. A lone fiddle bow danced frenetically in its player's hand as it rubbed loud, clear, appealing notes from its violin's strings through a series of photos of the happy times in the 1950s. Life appeared good then, as photo after photo showed smiling, happy people working and playing in town. On cue, a loud vocalist added the human voice to the lively mix.

The post-World War II photos came and then the show ended with the pictures revealing the area as seen today in the twenty-first century. By this time, the crowd was ready for it to end. Throughout the show, some watchers were noticeably quiet when the picture of a passed loved one came up, but loudly laughed with others at the recent photos of those still living. The musicians and narrators were given a rousing, standing ovation when it was over.

SOMETIME THE FOLLOWING WEEKEND, Dosh met Reggie in Anderson's Grocery.

"What the hell," he said, "only two pictures. Only two pictures from the rez. Uncle Zim and that old one of Buffalo. I thought you said there would be more."

"Hey," his friend answered. "Whaddya want? At least there were two. Don't get greedy."

"For Christ's sake," Dosh went on, giving a quick glance to the nearby check-out girl, and lowering his voice. "What about the rest? What about now?"

"The rest? Now?" Reggie asked as he lifted the sack of groceries and snugged them into the crook of his arm. "Come by the office someday, and I'll show them to you," he said with laughter.

175

He hurried out the store, saying he had to get going. Dosh stood momentarily, watching his friend through the large store window. Deep in thought, he reached to his shirt pocket, removed the short grocery list, and walked through the few isles, searching for the list's items.

On Monday, Dosh went about his work at the tribal fish hatchery as usual. He measured the tiny pellets of dry food for the trout fingerlings and carefully dropped them into the water at the scheduled feeding times. He did the regular work with the young walleye as well, selecting a fingerling from the designated samples to do the routine checks to monitor its growth and health. He enjoyed his work with the fish, enjoyed especially the trips with the tank trucks when the fish were big enough to be released into the region's lakes and streams. Over the last several years, he had been part of the crews that released thousands and thousands of fish into those waters.

But this morning, he struggled with the musical photo show. Two images remained before him. *Two pictures,* he kept thinking. *Out of the entire hour and a half we got two damn pictures.*

Finally, late in the afternoon when his work was completed, he could wait no longer. When on his daily afternoon trip to tribal headquarters to pick up the mail, he hurried downstairs to Reggie's office.

"All right," he said, "where're the rest of those pictures?"

"Hey, Dosh," Reggie said. He leaned over to reach the switch on his computer and, after turning it off, rose from behind his desk. "Come-on," he continued. "Look at these." He opened a brown folder to expose a stack of black-and-white pictures, all enlarged copies. Some were grainy with age, while a few were from originals that had obviously come from posed studio portraits. The folder held only a small sample of the many Reggie had been gathering over the past year.

Dosh took several into his hands, one after another, briefly studying them. "Boy," he muttered in surprise, "where'd you get all these?"

"Here and there. Some are copies from old newspapers, some from the BIA, some from the Smithsonian, and some from the church in town. There should be lots more showing up. I've only started on this. I get to it when I can."

"Waah," Dosh exclaimed, "this has to be Lettie Gurneaux when she was just a kid. Look at her! Look at that old house!"

"Hey, come on. You can see these later. I want you to meet our new staff land worker. She just came on board yesterday. Come on," he motioned as he moved to the door. "She's upstairs."

Dosh followed his friend up to the main floor, past the receptionist and into a hallway that led to the rear of the building. Reggie walked into a small office at the end of the corridor that had "ZONING" painted on its door.

"Sue, do you remember this guy?" Reggie asked an attractive young woman peering into a monitor screen behind a desk.

"Dosh?" she asked, extending a hand.

"Sue?" he answered, "Sue Morrisson?"

"That's right," she said. "How long has it been?"

The two renewed their friendship, one that went back to the fifth grade at St. Isadore's in town. Now well into their thirties, they started remembering old incidents, old joys—all with laughter.

But Reggie, always efficient and in a hurry, would not let them continue. "Hey," he interrupted. "Sue, show Dosh what you've been working on, what you told me this morning."

Sue Morrison, brown haired, slender, and in an almost plain or common way, was an attorney with years of work in real-estate law. Following a divorce, she was enticed to come back after over a twenty-five-year absence. Some felt it was the nice salary the tribe offered, money from the new casino downstate, but others knew she came home after too many years in cities. Her return brought the old rez name— Morrisson—back. No Morrissons had lived on the rez since her dad moved the family to Cleveland long since. Whatever it was, she was digging in and seemed to have a passion for her work.

Dosh heard of her return, but until today had not tracked her down. It had been long ago, and people change.

177

"Oh, I'm working on land recovery. Hopefully, I'll find ways to help the tribe get its land back," she stated.

"Back?" Dosh said.

"Yah, you know, just like at White Earth. They've been working on it for years. They're buying some back and going to court to litigate for the return of parcels taken illegally," she went on.

"Wow," Dosh continued, "heavy. You mean we're gonna get the land back—get the rez back into Indian hands?"

"That's the goal. Long term, but that's the idea. The tribal council is all gung-ho for it," Sue said.

"I'll be damned," Dosh uttered quietly as a look came over him that told of something good happening inside.

LATER THAT DAY, AFTER WORK, Dosh left the hatchery and turned his pick-up truck onto County Road Z instead of heading right home. The blacktop wound into the woods behind the outdoor rearing ponds and found the high ground as it looped north for two miles before turning east then south back to the reservation village. It was a stretch of reservation roadway still completely in forest and was sought after by the color worshippers from downstate each October. The maples, oaks, and aspens, with their oranges, reds, and yellows put on a show the tourists loved.

The groves of oaks were also good hunting territory when the acorns started to ripen and fall. Dosh never failed to take his share of venison from the miles of ridge along County Z, but the ridge's high ground also afforded the onlooker a spectacular view of the big lake and its islands. Just to the south, beside the lake was the village, then further south, again beside the lake, was the town. It was marked by two chimneys of the plywood plant and the four white church spires above the tree line, pointing to their heaven.

The blue waters below, off in the distance, were eye-catching. Today Dosh was filled with images and thoughts of the last few weeks.

The tanks of healthy walleye, lake and brook trout he helped rear all year pleased him. His cousin Reggie pleased him. The return of Sue Morrisson pleased him. But this pleasure was countered by a creeping feeling of discomfort. That musical booster show in the gym would not leave him. "Two pictures," he kept saying to himself as he slowly drove along. "Only two. And the land," he muttered aloud.

Today he stopped his truck on the road's gravel shoulder, turned the ignition off, opened the door and stepped down. He stood on the blacktop and in a few long steps was through the ditch and into the woods. Proceeding only about twenty yards, he selected an oak, walked to it and reached into a rear jeans pocket to withdraw a leather tobacco pouch. Unzipping it, he carefully reached in with thumb and index finger and removed a good-sized pinch.

Then he bent to place the tobacco at the base of the tree.

SUMMER ENDED AND, WITH THE ONSET of fall, Dosh was busy with the hatchery crew as it pumped young fish into truck tanks and transported them to three regional inland lakes. The walleye had been hatched from roe taken during spring's spearing season. The eggs were fertilized with sperm milked from the males, then reared in the indoor tanks. This circling regeneration of fish pleased him.

Reggie was busy as well. He covered the town's annual Apple Festival in early October, shooting photographs and even writing a lengthy article for an urban newspaper in the far, southern portion of the state. It seemed to Dosh that Reggie's journalism career was starting to go somewhere. Somehow a rumor was started in the village that Reggie was thinking of having a reservation Squash Festival next year as a fundraiser for the youth. As if he wasn't busy enough.

Some tribal members joked about a Squash Festival as they wondered about how the people gardened long ago. They knew stories of squashes, pumpkins, rutabagas, carrots, and cabbages. Gardening had been big back then. Dosh saw all that in Reggie's folders of photos.

Dosh was at the hatchery, thinking of all this late one morning in early November when Reggie phoned. He said he was coming by to show him something.

He watched through the small window in the hatchery office building as his cousin drove into the dirt parking lot and hurried inside, a sheaf of papers clutched in one hand.

"Look at this," Reggie said, handing the papers across the desk to his cousin. "Sue found it yesterday over at the Register of Deeds Office. It's a competency certificate."

"A certificate of competency? For who?" Dosh asked, taking the paper.

"Angeliquekwe LaRiche. She was Uncle Zim's mother. Isn't it neat?—so patriotic—all that scrollwork, those flags and eagles?" Reggie went on.

"'To All Who Read These Presents, Greetings—,'" Dosh started reading. "'Let it be known that Angeliquekwe LaRiche, an Ojibwe allottee, Number 2174, is hereby found to be of sound mind and body and therefore is deemed competent to handle her own affairs.'"

"Ya," Reggie interjected. "D'ja ever see one of these?"

"Nope," Dosh replied. "Aren't they awful? As if she were a child or something."

"Hey, that's not all. Sue says there might be more."

Dosh looked up and said, "What?"

"Well, do you know where her allotment was?"

"No," Dosh replied.

"At Clam Bay—it included most of the shoreline."

"So? Right where the marina is?"

"That's right. That whole chunk of land running back from the lake was once the old LaRiche farm back in the 1880s after the logging."

Dosh, still puzzled, said, "So what does Sue say about it?"

"Well," Reggie said, "this might be good. She said she's been working on this most of the week. She traced the changes of ownership from the present owners right back to Uncle Zim's ma. It was sold to different ones until the Johnsons got it back in the 1970s and built the marina. She says the LaRiches apparently never paid any taxes on it, so the county took it in 1914. They sold it to a white man the same year."

Dosh knew about the Competency Act of 1906 and how the county had confiscated many reservation land parcels after tribal members took the certificates so they could log their allotments. Since the lands were taxable, they had to start paying real estate taxes, but many, for whatever reasons, did not.

"Don't you get it?" Reggie asked, excitedly.

"What?" Dosh replied, still unsure what he was up to.

"Uncle Zim. It's about Uncle Zim. Sue says she found where the county said there were no heirs who could have had a chance to pay the taxes, so it took the land. But there was Uncle Zim. He must have been in his mid-twenties in 1916. He wasn't killed until 1918. He was an heir, and he was alive when the county took the land."

"So," Dosh slowly said, "that means the Johnson's don't have clear title to the marina? That means all these years that still was tribal land? But, Uncle Zim was killed, and he had no children."

"That's what Sue's working on. She thinks that because he was alive when the land was taken, the confiscation was illegal. Uncle Zim should have been given the chance to pay those back taxes. Whether he could have or would have is immaterial. She thinks he was never given the chance—that the county went ahead, took the land and turned right around and sold it. She found a deed in the name of Thomas Swenson, maybe the lumberyard people over in Ashland, dated March 12, 1917. Paperwork with the confiscation says the county found no heirs."

Dosh took his eyes from the certificate of competency and raised them to meet the excited gaze of his cousin. "So . . . so," he slowly said, "what's Sue goin' to do?"

"She's been on the Net for days, looking for any precedents. And she's talking with some lawyer friends in D.C. about her next step."

"Geez," Dosh muttered, a smile crossing his face.

"Hey," Reggie said, taking the papers back as he moved to the door. Turning to his cousin before hurrying out to his truck, he added, "and she's only started. This was the first parcel she looked at."

LATER, WHEN FINISHED WITH HIS WORK, Dosh again took the blacktop loop home. The trees had given up their leaves, and the view was even more spectacular. Stopping and again entering the woods, he stood beside the oak. He noted the town way off in the distance, its plywood mill with dirty-looking steam rising from its two smoke stacks. They pointed upward in a fashion like the church steeples. Closer he studied the much smaller reservation village. He easily saw the tribal headquarters, the bingo hall, the other tribal buildings, and the small houses and many trailer homes, nestled among the leafless trees.

All this lay beside the big lake, he thought, as if paying homage to it. Then suddenly he felt the familiar good feelings of home. He liked the view, the water, the islands. He liked the way the forest regenerated itself from the ruthless devastation of the clear-cutting almost a hundred years before, the carnage shown in many of Reggie's old photographs. He thought of the young walleye growing down in the hatchery's rearing ponds and of the others he helped release into the wild. And he thought of Sue Morrisson.

Most important, amidst all this, he imagined the dusky image of a man he never met. That late November afternoon, Dosh saw Uncle Zim on the ridge beside him, standing bigger than life, towering above it all. In his old World War I olive-drab uniform, he stood with arms akimbo, silently looking down on the rez, smiling at the big lake and its dark islands.

℘ • ℜ

Source of Chapter Opening Quotations

Kittredge, William, *Owning It All*, 1987, Greywolf Press, St. Paul.

De Montaigne, Michel, *Essays*, 1958 (1580), Penguin Books, England.

Perry, Michael, *Off Main Street*, 2005, Harper Collins, New York.

Nelson, Richard, *The Island Within*, 1989, Douglas & McIntrye, Vancouver.

Abbey, Edward, *Earth Apples*, 1994, St. Martin's Press, New York.

Maugham, W. Somerset, *Of Human Bondage*, 1992 (1915), Penguin, New York.

Kafka, Franz, *The Basic Kafka*, 1979, Pocket Books, New York.

Van Stappen, Michael, *Northern Passages*, 1998, Prairie Oak Press, Madison.

Beston, Henry, *The Outermost House*, 1992 (1928), Henry Holt, New York.

Williams, Terry Tempest, *An Unspoken Hunger*, 1994, Vintage Books, New York.

Eiseley, Loren, *The Lost Notebooks of Loren Eiseley*, 1987, Little Brown, Boston.

Meyers, Kent, *The Witness of Combines*, 1998, University of Minnesota Press, Minneapolis.

Nelson, Rodney, *Villy Sadness*, 1987, New Rivers Press, St. Paul.

Lueders, Edward, *The Clam Lake Papers*, 1977, Abingdon, Nashville.

Treuer, David, *Little*, 1997, Graywolf Press, St. Paul.

Wub-e-ke-niew, *We Have The Right to Exist*, 1995, Black Thistle Press, New York.

Matthiessen, Peter, *At Play in the Fields of the Lord*, 1991 (1965), Vintage Books, New York.

Wub-e-ke-niew, *We Have the Right to Exit*, 1995, Black Thistle Press, New York.

Peacock, Thomas and Marlene Wisuri, *Waasa Inaabidaa*, 2002, Afton Historical Society Press, Afton.